THE ROYAL YORKER'S DAUGHTER

JaCol Publishing Inc.

FIRST PRINTING

December 2019

JaCol Publishing Inc.
195 Murica Aisle
Irvine, CA 92614
818-510-2898
Editor-in-Chief: Randall
Andrews
www.jacolpublishing.com
ISBN: 978-1-946675-36-1

ACKNOWLEDGEMENT

For my great grandfather, Private Ananias Archer, and all the Heroes of our War for Independence. For Mrs. Cannon, my Jr. high English teacher, who instilled a love of reading and writing in a country boy, and for my patient wife, Geraldine Yerdon Archer

I'd also like to thank my editor, Randall Andrews, and my cover artist Karen Edwards.

Table of Contents

Chapter 1

Only the foolish believe wars are a path to glory. There is no glory in death or defeat, nor even glory in winning. In the end, only suffering and death followed by preparation for the next battle, the next war exists. My father, Tiberius Morrissey, experienced the worst of war at Fort Carillon. They brought him home more dead than alive, and his recovery took longer than a year.

My parents hoped I would become a doctor, lawyer, or an important government official, but my father always said I would probably be a farmer, the same as he. I was a baby when my four-year-old sister, Julia, died from what mother said was the *Great Throat Disruption.* I was sick as well, but I survived as their only living child. I believe mother mourned Julia until the day she became a grandmother and held baby Rebecca in her arms.

I have no memory of the war with the French, but my father had been a Captain in the militia and told me stories about his experiences. He warned me, "Battle changes a man. It rips at your heart and your mind." He always ended the stories with the same words, "I hope you never have to experience war.

In 1761, two years after the victories at Niagara and Carillon, Quebec had been taken, the French had been thrown out of Canada, and England emerged victorious around the globe. The final peace remained elusive for another two years, but in Tryon County, life was already peaceful, and the Militia only trained occasionally. There were no alarms, no marches, no fighting, and the corn on our farm was green, tall and tasseled out.

My father resigned his commission in the militia because of lingering effects from his wounds and devoted his efforts to farming and raising a boy who worshipped him. By the time I was four, I had regular chores and I often went with my father and the oxen. I remember sometimes he would put me up on one of them to ride.

Shortly after my father had resigned from the militia, I listened to him and my mother talk about the man who would be the new Captain, William Campbell. "Who is he, Tiberius, and why did he get the job instead of Lieutenant MacGregor?" She asked.

"He has a brother who is married to a relative of Sir William. That's probably why he was picked for the position. That and the fact that he was an officer in the 42nd Regiment of Foot. I believe he will do a fine job, Martha."

"What else do you know about him?"

"Not a lot. He was badly wounded at Carillon. The 42nd fought like demons, and they paid a heavy price for it."

"Is he here already?"

"Not yet. He is still straightening up his affairs, and selling his house."

"Where will he live?"

"According to Colonel Johnson, he is going to try to hire carpenters here to build a house for him and his family. He wants to be settled in before winter."

"He will have to arrive soon then, or it will be too late to get it done. He will have to have lumber sawed as well."

"The lumber is being sawed for him right now, and I am going to see if I can get a job with him. I'm a pretty good carpenter."

****

Captain Campbell was well liked in the militia and our community, and my father enjoyed working on his house. He got to know the Captain reasonably well, and they occasionally reminisced about the battle of Carillon that had nearly claimed both their lives.

Father ended up supervising the other builders, mostly militia members who were used to taking orders from him. He took me with him from time to time, and compared to our little home, the new house was magnificent. It was completed before the first snow fell, and the Captain was pleased with the finished structure. He agreed to hire my father to begin clearing his land in the spring, so I would see the Campbell's from time to time when I went with him.

They had two children, George, who was about 4 years older than me, and a daughter, Ellie, who was 2 years my junior. Actually her name was Elspeth, but everyone except her mother called her Ellie. George and I became good friends and spent a lot of happy hours together.

By the time I was 6, I actually helped with the oxen, leading them, cleaning and grooming them, feeding them, and once in a while working them pulling a small stump. By the time I was 12, I often spelled my father and worked the team on my own under my father's supervision. I didn't mind being a farmer.

Chapter 2

A Successful Hunt

I hunted rabbits, squirrels, and turkeys with George from the time I was ten, but what I really wanted to do was hunt deer and bear. He didn't seem to pick up on the hints I dropped at every opportunity. Finally I just flat out told him, "I think I'm old enough to go deer hunting."

"I think you are too. When the weather cools down and the deer are fat, we will do it."

We went a couple times in September, but we came back emptyhanded. We saw two or three but never close enough to take a shot. We didn't have many chances to hunt, because he was preparing to become a solicitor's clerk. His father wanted him to learn law, and George was more than happy to get such an opportunity.

It was a crisp October day when George told me, "I'll be leaving soon for Connecticut to work for a solicitor and learn law, but I'd like to go hunting with you one more time before I leave, but this time for deer. The acorns and chestnuts are falling. We might get a deer or at least a turkey if you could go tomorrow."

That night, I broached the hunt with my father, "George says the deer and turkeys are feeding on acorns, and he is going hunting tomorrow. He asked me to go with him. Do I have to work, or can I go?"

Yes, you can go. Take my rifle, not the musket. A turkey would taste good. You probably won't get a deer, but at least with the rifle you will have a better chance if you see one. Remember, aim close."

My mother had breakfast ready early when a knock came at the door. "Hello George," she said, "have you had your breakfast?"

"Yes, I have."

"Would you like an egg or slice of toast for a snack? I have some extra all made and I can pack some for both of you. That might taste good a little later."

I answered for him, "That would be great mother. A guy can work up an appetite hunting."
We cleared the leaves away from under our feet so they wouldn't accidentally rustle and alert a deer or turkey. We finished the food before the sun was barely up. For the first hour or so, neither turkeys nor deer came for the acorns that littered the ground. I whispered, "Maybe we are in the wrong spot."

"I don't think so. It's early yet. We just have to be patient. I know the turkeys have been coming through here, so they will most likely be back again. It's their nature."

The sun crept higher in the East. Frost glistened on the trees until the warm rays touched it. A blue jay scolded something in the distance and squirrels busied themselves collecting nuts while we watched them. The woods were becoming noisy as the squirrels ran through the brittle leaves. "Deer would never hear us now," George commented.

My hopes had already evaporated like the morning frost, when a deer appeared magically under the oak trees. "I see a deer, George."

He resisted the urge to look, and sat absolutely still. He cautioned me, "Remember, don't move and don't try to raise your gun until his head is turned away or behind a tree."

My mouth dried, I couldn't swallow, and I felt like I had to cough. I could feel my heart thumping against my ribs. I cocked my rifle; it sounded like a limb cracking, but the deer didn't hear it. I raised my gun waiting for a clear shot. The suspense must have been hard for my friend to bear, and he jumped when the rifle cracked.

"Did you get him?"

"I don't know. I aimed right behind his shoulder, but he ran off over the hill."

"That doesn't mean anything; a deer can run a hundred yards shot clear through the lungs or the heart. Come on, let's go look. Just where was he when you shot?"

"He was right over to the left of those two big oaks. I raised my gun when he went behind them, but he took forever to walk out. I'm sure I was on him."

George kept his eyes on the ground until we came to the spot where the deer had stood. He bent over and picked up a tuft of deer hair. "You hit him, Jacob, watch for blood."

Tracking the deer was no problem as small red pools marked his path, and we saw him lying on the ground ahead of us. I whooped like an Indian and ran to the dead deer, a buck with a small set of antlers.

"Great shot! Now the work begins. First open him up. A deer is no different from a squirrel or a rabbit, he's just bigger, and be careful not to cut into the stomach or things will be a mess." He leaned against a tree and watched me.

I had no problem, I had helped my father with a beef, and there was little difference other than I was doing this alone. When I came to the heart, I removed it and poked my finger into the bullet hole, holding it up for George to see.

"You can't do any better than that. He didn't suffer much. He was dead before he hit the ground." George, put his thumb into the deer blood and then wiped a streak across my forehead. "You may be only 12 years old, but you have killed a deer, and the Indians would say you are a man."

It was nearly noon when we got the deer to the homestead, but tired as I was, I could hardly wait to brag about my feat. "I got a deer mother!"

I took her outside. "Isn't he a good one? I got him right through the heart too."

"He certainly is a beauty. You and George should skin him, cut him into quarters and hang them up in the smoke house. The flies won't bother them there, and it's cold enough now that it will age fine before we cut him up. Did you save the heart and liver?"

"Yes. I have them on a stick inside his chest to keep them clean."

"Well get them for me and I'll take them inside. We will have bacon and liver tomorrow night. George do you want half of the liver?"

"No. My father isn't fond of liver of any kind."

"Would you like some of the meat when we butcher it?"

"I will probably be gone to Connecticut by then, but I'm sure mother and father would appreciate getting some."

"I'll take some over for them. We wouldn't have any if George hadn't taken me."

That was the first of many deer I would shoot, but I will always remember that one best. I remember how proud I was to show my father the venison hanging in the smoke house.

"You've done yourself proud, son. Now there is one thing left to do. It's time you learned the proper way to clean a rifle or a musket. I've always done it for you, but you have seen how. You should always do it as soon as you can. Take good care of your gun, and it will always take care of you.

Chapter 3

Tiberius

The northern New York wilderness changed from forest to farm land, cleared tree by tree and stump by stump. Tryon County grew and prospered after the war with the French. It seemed like we were free from troublesome politics and the threat of war. Ellie and I grew up in a time of peace.

London was 3400 miles across the Atlantic, Boston was 320 miles on the East Coast, and New York City 290 miles south. At first, the King and his minions had minimal effect on us and our county, but between the time of our births and 1775, events took place that radically changed our lives and our world.

****

Tiberius stopped the oxen and sat down on the plow breathing heavily. He looked at me. "You are going to have to take over. I don't know what ails me."

My spine buzzed, like a lightning rod just before a thunder storm, and goose bumps marched across my arms. I heard my father speak, but my attention was elsewhere. I put my trigger finger to my lips and strained my ears for the slightest sound. I looked around for the source of my uneasiness.

"What is it? What's the matter? Walk on the other side of the oxen and drop into that low spot that's up ahead. You'll be able to move out of sight and around behind that rise. If there is someone, it must be where they are."

I crept on my hands and knees and circled the possible hiding place, using the depression and grass for cover. I had to resist the temptation to look too soon, but when I ran out of concealment, I looked up. I had been right. I closed in without making a sound.

My father looked in my direction when I stood up holding a kicking, screaming Ellie around her waist. He appeared amused by the sight, but he was probably relieved as much as anything. She shouted, "Put me down, Jacob Morrissey. If I tell my father you grabbed me, you will be in big trouble."

Obviously she had been surprised. I let her feet settle back on the ground and turned her around holding her shoulders. "What were you doing spying on us all the way out here? Do your parents know where you are?"

She pulled loose from my grasp, stepped back, straightening her dress, and breathing hard, she replied,

"My mother does, and I wasn't spying. I was just watching you work."

"Well, you could have stood up and watched us, you didn't have to hide behind the bushes."

"I was watching you, not your father, but I didn't want you to know. You haven't come over to our home since George went to Hartford, and I miss seeing you and so does father."

"He has been gone for some time, and I have been busy, but I don't believe your father cares if I come or not."

"You are wrong. My father thinks a great deal of you, and I'm sure he would like to tell you how well George is doing, but you could come just to see me."

I scratched my head and smiled. "Well, Ellie, I just might do that, stop over to see your father and talk, about George that is."

For just a moment, a little scowl clouded her face before she chirped, "I'd better get home and let you get back to work."

She skipped away downhill through the spring grass, and twice she turned her head and looked back at me before I returned to father. He grinned and asked, "What was that all about?"

"It was that crazy Ellie Campbell, she was just watching us. She told me I should stop over to see her father and let him tell me about George. I don't know why."

"What are you so upset about? That doesn't seem like such a horrible thing. Are you going to go?"

"I don't know, probably, but she is such a pest. She said I should come and see her too. I told you she was crazy.

He didn't reply. His smile evaporated and he started to tremble, startling me.

"Are you all right, father? You look terrible."

He turned back toward the oxen, his face ashen, and grabbed onto the plow, before he slipped to the ground. His only words were, "Go get the horse, I can't walk." His eyes closed. I called his name, but I couldn't rouse him. I hated to leave him, but I had to go for help.

The newly plowed ground made running difficult, but I ran anyway, kicking up clods and stumbling over others. I made it to the unplowed meadow and ran the rest of the way without stopping. When the barn and cabin were in sight, I found new energy and charged into the yard shouting, "Mother! Mother! Father needs help!

She burst out of the cabin door. "What happened? Is he hurt?"

"I don't know what happened. One moment he was laughing and talking and the next he fell to the ground and passed out. Just before, he told me to get the horse."

"Hitch Silas to the wagon. He probably can't ride."

I startled poor old Silas with my rush to get his collar on and get him out of the barn. He stomped his feet in protest. He was used to being used more gently and getting a carrot or piece of maple sugar before harnessing, and he seemed determined to remind me. As hard as it was, instead of being irritated, I calmed down and spoke softly to him. The resistance subsided, and he allowed me to lead him out to the wagon and finish my task.

Mother was more thoughtful than I had been and gave the horse a piece of maple before she climbed into the wagon. I got in beside her and slapped the reins lightly on Silas's back. There was a sudden lurch, but then the horse settled into a steady trot. I avoided the direct route over the plowed ground, saving on horse and body, but the longer time it took seemed like an eternity.

When I turned the wagon toward the oxen, I had hoped I would see father sitting up or perhaps even standing. Instead, I saw him lying in the same crumpled heap. I drove the horse beyond father and the oxen and brought him to a halt.

Mother jumped off before I stopped and knelt down beside my father. She lifted his head into her lap, listened for breathing and felt for a pulse. She let his head rest back on the ground, bent over and put her ear against his chest. "He's alive. Help me get him into the wagon."

I picked him up, not needing her help, and put him in the wagon. "I'll ride in the box with him, Jacob."

"Where should we take him? Home?"

"No, I think we should take him directly to Dr. Wright's home. He might not be there, but we can't ride all over looking for him. I'll pray he will be there or get there soon." She held his head in her lap. "I'm going to keep his head from bumping against the hard floor."

"I'll try to miss as many holes and bumps as I can, but the rutted road will still be a hard ride. I'll go slowly to keep it from being too bad.

I reined Silas in outside the doctor's home, jumped down and pounded on the door.

Dr. Wright opened it. "Don't knock my door down, Jacob. What's the problem?"

"It's my father. He's in the wagon. He passed out plowing."

He looked at my father. "Can you carry him into my office?"

"Just show me where you want me to put him."

I placed him on a small bed, he felt cold to the touch. "Would you put a blanket over him?"

"I will as soon as I finish examining him. Now would you and your mother please sit in the other room while I see if I can figure out what is going on?"

The minutes seemed to drag on forever before the door opened and the doctor came in.

"How is he doctor? Do you know what's wrong with him? Can you help him?

"One question at a time Mrs. Morrissey. I need some information first. Has your husband been ill lately?"

"Not sick really, but a time or two he said he was too tired to work. That's not like him."

"Did he say anything else about how he felt when he was tired?"

"Not that I can remember. He would just settle down and take a nap."

"Well he is resting quietly, but that doesn't mean he is going to be fine. He hasn't regained consciousness yet, and his breathing is ragged at times. I believe he has either had a heart attack, or more likely a stroke. It would not surprise me from what you have said that he might have had a small stroke or maybe two before today. There is not much I can do for him right now except keep him warm and comfortable. I will keep track of him tonight. Until he is conscious, I will not be able to assess the full extent of his affliction, but I don't want to mislead you, his condition is serious."

Chapter Four

On Their Own

The community turned out in tribute to Tiberius, sharing my pain and grief. The sun couldn't warm me as I stared numbly at the pine box and the mound of freshly turned earth, stark against the green grass.

A soft hand took my own. Ellie stood there, tears running down her face. "Oh Jacob, I'm so sorry. He looked so well when he was plowing the other day. My mother and father are waiting for me, but I wanted you to know I was here for you."

Watching her walk away, his mother commented, "She's a fine young lady."

"She's a little girl, mother. She's only thirteen."

"It was thoughtful of her to come all the same. The Campbell's have been good friends. They all like you." We watched Ellie catch up with her parents, and her father waved goodbye.

"Come Jacob," she put her hand on my shoulder. "Let the men do their job, we can do him no good standing here."

"What are we going to do now, mother?"

"We will survive without your father. We saved some money, and we have our livestock and our land. Thank the good Lord that Sir William granted the land freely to your father for his heroic service in the war. We pay no rent, but we must look for jobs to earn some hard cash, you might find work for the oxen, but most of our needs will be covered by our harvest, and I will sell butter and eggs."

"I will always take care of you mother, have no fear of that. But what if people say I am too young to do the work?"

"Your father taught you how to use the oxen, and he told me you were doing most of the work. Now is the time to put that skill to use. People will pay well for the services of our oxen. There is always land to be cleared. You are big for your age and nearly as strong as the oxen; I don't think anyone will question you, and don't hesitate to ask for the same wages as your father received. He was fair and if you do as good a job as your father did, you will be worth every shilling."

"Father took goods and credit for wages many times, and he knew what he was doing. He always did well in the end."

"You can do that too, but as often as possible, get actual coins. If we are careful and thrifty, there is a chance you may become a doctor or a lawyer, someone important. Now let's go home and pray for wisdom from the Lord and His leading."

Someone knocked at the door that afternoon. I opened it and George waited with a loaf of fresh baked bread. "Afternoon, Jacob. Mother baked this for you and your mother, and my father wants to know if there is anything he can do for you."

I turned to mother; she smiled and nodded. I invited George in. "Yes there is. You know my father had been clearing your land, and I believe he wants to clear another section this year. My father was expecting to be hired again, but now that he is gone, your father will need someone else. Would you put in a good word for me? I can do the job just about as well as my father could."

"I'm sure you can. I know you worked the oxen for some time now. You are right; he is planning on clearing another section this year, and he is already wondering who he could get to finish it. Do you think you could clear a whole section by yourself?"

My enthusiasm surfaced. "I'm sure I can. I'll do a great job too."

"I'm leaving for Connecticut day after tomorrow. I can't be away from the office too long, but I'll see what I can do. Come to the house tonight after dinner, and my father will discuss it with you, but before I go, may I ask what do you expect to charge?"

"I am going to ask for the same wages he paid my father."

"I hoped you would, but I believe he will try to hire you for less, stand your ground, and I'll put in a good word for you, but I can't promise anything. See you tonight."

When George was gone, I turned to mother. "Can you believe it? I was hoping I might find some work with the Captain, but now perhaps I will have work for all summer."

"Nothing is ever sure, you have George on your side, but it will be up to you to make a case for yourself. It will be important for him to see you are confident you can do the job."

That afternoon I planned what I would say to Mr. Campbell, but somehow my words sounded more like a speech than a conversation. Mother listened to me until dinner time. "For goodness sake, you're not going to see a stranger. Speak to him, but be yourself. Be polite and let him do most of the talking. He knows how old you are. Just make sure you are confident and don't be afraid to ask for a fair wage."

Dinner ended and I champed at the bit to get on my way before dark. "Wish me luck mother. I'll do my best to get the job."

That evening, I made my way to their farm and Ellie opened the door when I knocked. "George told me you were coming tonight. Father is expecting you. Come into the library with me."

"Come in Jacob, come in," Mr. Campbell welcomed me. "I am so very sorry for your loss. Your father was a considerate, dependable man, wise in all things, and a good friend. I will miss him very much."

"Thank you, sir. I know he held you in high regard as well. He often said you were the best and fairest man he had ever worked for."

"Well, George tells me you are looking for work for your oxen. I was going to have your father clear a section for me this year, but now I have to find someone else. Mr. Tarbell has already inquired about the job, but I haven't made a decision."

Not to discredit Mr. Tarbell, but I can do the job for you, sir. I can clear the whole section for you this season. I may be young, but I know the work and the oxen are the same ones my father used."

"And what would you require for wages?"

"I am asking the same payment that you gave my father."

"But he was experienced and the head of a family. Why should you get the same as he did?

"Because I did much of his work, especially when he was tired or his leg acted up."

"How do I know you will finish the job? I will give you three quarters of what I paid your father.

"I want to work for you, but I am the head of my family now. If I complete the section, pay me his wages, if I fail to finish the job, you may pay me what you think I was worth, but I am confident that you will be satisfied."

"You drive a hard bargain, but a workman is worth his hire, and if you are three quarters the man your father was, I'll get the bargain. Tarbell wanted more, but even with his son, Simon, I don't believe he could finish the job in one season."

Before I could thank him, Ellie jumped up and down, "Thank you, father. Thank you. I've seen him working, and he's the best. You won't be sorry."

"I'm sure I won't be. Now why don't the two of you skedaddle to the kitchen and see if there are some sweets to go with a cup of tea."

In the kitchen, Ellie held both of my hands. She had to look up, because I was so much taller than her. "Isn't it wonderful, Jacob? Now I will get to see more of you. You will have to come to dinner sometimes, and to my birthday party. I'm going to be 14. Did you know my mother married my father when she was 15? Well, she did, and she says it was the best thing she ever did."

I turned her hands loose. "You had better put the tea kettle on before your father wonders what has happened to us."

Ellie's mother came into the kitchen. "Elspeth, what's going on? I heard you talking away about dinners and birthday parties."

"Father sent us to put the kettle on and find some sweets. He has just agreed to hire Jacob to clear the new section, and we are celebrating."

"I see. Jacob, why don't you go back to the library with my husband, and Elspeth and I will bring in the tea."

<h1 style="text-align:center">Chapter Five</h1>

While we waited for our tea, Mr. Campbell asked, "When can you start?"

"I can start tomorrow, "Our plowing is done, and our oats are in, but it's too early to plant corn, there is no reason I can't do it."

"You are an eager one. I like that in a man. You certainly are your father's son. Why don't you plan on having lunch with us tomorrow and you can let us know how it is going, and if you need anything?"

"Thank you, sir. I will be here early in the morning."

When I got home, mother asked, "How did it go?"

"It went wonderfully well. I got the job, and I start tomorrow. He is going to pay me the same as father."

Next morning, I ate breakfast before the sun peeked over the horizon, and planned to pull five stumps in the morning on my first day. The oxen had complained at being yoked so early and moved at the only speed they knew—slow. They could uproot even the largest stumps. No one owned a stronger team than mine, and three stumps lie on the ground when Ellie showed up with water and a sweet bun.

"Thanks Ellie, but you didn't need to do this."

"Yes I did," she said, "Momma sent me out. She asked me to tell you not to forget lunch."

She slid her hand over my arm and ran back toward home.

I smiled.

Mother is right, she is very nice, but she is still a little girl.

I pulled two more stumps before lunch, and four more after for a total of nine stumps. Not a bad day for one man and two oxen, but one short of my goal. The team struggled with large tree stumps that had substantial roots, and they were visibly exhausted. If I tried to pull more stumps, they might be too stiff and sore in the morning to work, but not all the stumps would be as large as those had been, and some days would produce better results.

I varied from my routine a few times—once for planting corn, and once for Ellie's birthday. She reminded me daily I had to come for her party, and I looked forward to her visits with water and a treat.

Martha insisted I wash my hair and clean up for the birthday. She also insisted I wear my best clothes. "It's a party, and it's in the Captain's home; you should look respectable."

George arrived home the day before Ella's birthday. He told me everyone except William had been surprised. It was good to see him again; we spent a couple hours catching up on what we both had been up to.

Two surplus roosters contributed to the festivities, and the chicken and biscuits was delicious.

Ellie told me, "I helped make dinner. I know it is my special day, but I wanted to do something just for you." She pretended not to see her mother's raised eyebrows.

"You certainly are a good cook. I don't know when I have had a meal any better."

After the cake, everyone moved to the parlor. She steered me to the sofa, and sat down beside me. She scowled when Caroline sat down on my other side. I think she disliked the way her friend eyed me and flirted with me. Caroline sat very close to me. When the time came for me to leave, Ellie walked to the door with me. "You said you were sorry you didn't have anything to give me for my birthday, but there is something, you can give me—a hug."

I was trapped. What would her family think? "Well," she pulled on my sleeve, "are you going to give me a hug for my birthday or not?"

I gingerly put my arms around her, but she grabbed my lapels and pulled me closer, giving me a kiss on the cheek like a cat marking its territory. She turned me loose. "Thanks for coming to my party. I'll see you tomorrow." She turned to Caroline and smiled.

George caught up with me outside. He said, "Hey, don't be in such a big hurry. I wanted to talk to you. I'm an apprentice solicitor now. I work at the office on a regular basis. You might want to think about joining me in Connecticut. I could help you."

"That's very generous of you, but I have mother and the farm now. I can't just leave everything behind."

"I understand, but think about it anyway. By the way, it looks to me like you have your hands full with Ellie. You know she has her cap set for you? Right?"

"She's just a little girl."

"A little girl she may be, but she is strong-willed and determined. She told mother that she was going to marry you. She won't give up easily. I just want you to know, if she has her way, I'll be a great brother-in-law."

****

I pulled twelve stumps one day and congratulated himself on a great job. I took a short, well-deserved break and scanned the piles of stumps and roots already dotting the field. I caught sight of someone walking toward me, too far away to identify. I could tell it was a man, and wondered who would be looking for me. Maybe someone who wanted to hire me. As the figure came closer, I made out Simon Tarbell. I was curious why he would come to see me in the field.

"Simon, what can I do for you?"

"You can get your oxen out of this field and go home."

"Why would I do that?"

"Because my father and I should be clearing this field. You cheated us out of the job. What did you do? Tell him you'd do the job cheaper than my father?"

"No, I only gave him a fair price. He liked the job my father and I had done for him, and he thought I could do as well."

"You need to leave while you can and your oxen aren't good only for beef."

He pulled out a large knife. "How much work will your team do with their tendons cut? Leave before I cut them and beat you senseless."

I moved, picked up my axe and placed myself between Simon and the oxen. I lifted the axe. "I've got a suggestion for you. Why don't you leave before I knock you down and chop off your hands? How much work will you do without hands? Drop that knife and leave."

Simon backed off but didn't drop the knife. He grinned with contempt. "I'll leave, but I'm not giving you my knife. There will be another time."

"No. Drop it or I'll take it." I held the axe with both hands, advancing toward the back peddling ruffian. I started to raise the axe, and Simon threw down the knife and ran.

I waited until Simon disappeared over the ridge, picked up the knife and made a mental note to keep a watch out for him. I didn't know how soon I would see him. My team and I were tired, and the oxen were very willing to head for home. A rivulet so small it had no name ran in the bottom of a shallow gully we crossed each day, and the oxen had made it a habit to stop and drink their fill before continuing on to the farm. I stopped, and allowed them to get their usual reward, but I was uneasy for some reason. I tossed it off as a reaction to the encounter with Simon. The oxen raised their heads when something struck me across my back. I stumbled forward and bumped into one of the animals. I was slightly stunned and I rolled to the left, off the ox, barely avoiding another blow that struck the poor animal instead. The team reacted to the blow by starting on their way home.

I revived the moment I fell into the cold spring water. I sprung up holding a rock in the palm of my hand. Simon rushed me, swinging a rough club. I ducked and slammed the rock into the side of his head. Simon dropped his club and stumbled, fell into the stream and held the left side of his head. I jumped on him and slammed the rock into his head again, this time to the right near his temple.

My adversary groaned and bled profusely, but he wasn't finished. Despite the two blows, he threw me off and grabbed at my leg. Before Simon could deliver any punishment, I rolled away, jumped up, and delivered a stiff kick to Simon's side, and then another. Ribs cracked. Putting my knee into Simons back, I grabbed his hair and pulled his head back and held Simon's knife in front of his eyes. "Do you want me to slit your throat before or after I scalp you?"

"No, you can't do that!"

"Yes I can. In the morning on my way to the Campbell's, I'll find your body here where the Indians left you. I'll have Mr. Campbell come and take you back to your father, and that will be that."

"No please, let me go. I'm sorry. I wasn't trying to kill you." I let go of his hair and stepped back.

Simon rose and bent over holding onto his side. His right eye was grotesquely swollen and bloody, his left ear looked like a fresh beef steak.

I gave him a warning. "I'll let you go, but if anything ever happens to my oxen, I'll hunt you down and kill you. Do you understand?"

"Yes, but how am I going to get home?"

"Walk, I suppose. Now get going. You've got a long trip to get back home before dark."

I watched Simon hobble away, but the results didn't feel like a victory. Instead, I felt sorry for Simon. His was a sad story, but that didn't excuse the mean things he did to others. No one likes a bully, and Simon was never well liked.

My back and neck hurt because of the blow from the club, and I let the oxen pull me along behind them as I walked.

After I finished feeding and bedding down the team, I walked to the house.

Mother said, "Your dinner is ready."

"I need to hitch up the wagon. I'll eat when I get back."

"What are you going to do? Why do you need the wagon?"

I told her about the encounters with Simon. "He is hurting badly. I can't let him walk all the way home. He might not make it."

"You've got a good heart. But be careful. You can never trust a wounded animal."

Chapter 6

1774-1775

The corn stood tall and green, ears well filled out. It had been a perfect growing season; the crop would be bountiful. It wasn't harvest season yet, but I was ready, nearly finished pulling stumps. I noticed Ellie had filled out like the ears of corn, and I looked forward to her visits in the field.

I surprised myself with the progress, and William was delighted. Misty smoke drifted over the Campbell farm from stumps burned into ash. The ashes would be turned into the soil by the spring plowing, and fertilize the ground with potash.

On the whole, life seemed good, the land was at peace, but recent rumblings beneath life's surface were growing louder and stronger. A political earthquake rumbled that would radically transform the world, and the only ones who could stop it were 3400 miles away without a clue.

We heard representatives from each colony were going to gather in Philadelphia, and try to relieve the colonies' complaints and restore tranquility. They were wise men. Certainly they could bring us safely through difficult times.

The first Continental Congress met in Philadelphia on September 5, 1774 to prepare a document for Parliament and the King, listing colonists' grievances. They penned resolutions, and hoped England would come to its collective senses, repealing the intolerable acts, and providing a pathway for Parliamentary representation from the new world.

On the whole, at least to me, it seemed like a reasonable proposal for redress, but we heard there were many among the delegates who believed the only solution was freedom for the colonies, and they were prepared, if necessary, to go to war to get it. On the other side of the Atlantic, this attempt to heal the wounds and acquire representation apparently met with ridicule, and contempt.

The news of the First Congress had reached Tryon County, arriving soon after I stored our corn in the crib. It was the talk of the village. Everyone had an opinion, and they were as diverse as the delegates'. Talk of freedom and war became more common

A Second Continental Congress was scheduled for May 1775, but events would overtake it. A pig-headed King, who would rather beat his subjects down than lift them up, hired Hessians to put down the annoying rebellion. "The die is cast." King George said after the Boston tea Party. He was not about to change his mind. The leaders waited for the king's reply. It would be long in coming and unsatisfactory.

****

Winter was unusually harsh in 1774–75. Blizzard after blizzard pounded the Northeast, and several Nor'easters made life miserable for residents on the coast. It was even worse in Boston. Not only were they suffering from the winter, but the king had closed the port to trade, and had sent several thousand soldiers, which by law, had to be quartered and fed by the Bostonians themselves. Indignation was strong and the people's temperament grew more militant as the days passed by and the soldiers devoured scarce food supplies.

The winter was just as cold and snowy in Tryon County as it was anywhere else, but most of its citizens were prepared to meet it head on.

"It's a good thing I put in a large supply of firewood this year, mother; keeping the cabin warm will use a lot."

"You predicted the winter would be extra hard with lots of snow. How did you know, Jacob?"

"The muskrat houses were piled extra high in the marsh, and the bears fed longer than usual before they denned. It made sense to me that if the animals were preparing for a hard winter, I should as well."

I was limited in the things I could do other than caring for our animals and keeping the fire going. I caught up on my reading when the weather was bitter, and on days when it moderated, I saddled the horse and visited Ellie. We sat in the parlor talking, sometimes saying nothing, just enjoying a cup of tea and a plate of scones that she had made herself. She snuggled up to me and took my arm, placing her hand on mine. She might have had an urge to kiss me, but she told me that after the display at the party, her mother had warned her not to be so forward. It was not ladylike. Ruth often appeared in the parlor and did needlework, pretending to be ignoring us.

The winter was having an effect on the well-to-do as much as on poor farmers. I'm sure Sir John and his family were comfortable in their big house, but they must have been looking for something to break up the monotony. They sent out announcements to important citizens, good friends, and nearby relatives that there was to be a ball held at Johnson Hall. The Campbell's had been invited to the dance, and Ellie was included.

She told me about the invitation and asked if I would go with her.

"I haven't gotten an invitation, and it's unlikely I will. We travel in different worlds, and I have no talent as a social climber, nor any desire to be one."

"What do you mean? Do you think my father is a social climber?"

"No. He is related somehow to the Johnsons and he is a captain in the militia under Sir Guy's command. He holds an acceptable social position, and more so because he is a relative."

"Do you think it is wrong to be well off?"

"No I don't. But I am far from being in the same class. I like your father, and I am happy for him and for you as well. You should all have a grand time, and then you can tell me all about it later."

Chapter 7

The Ball

The invitation surprised Jacob. He handed it to his mother. She said, "I'll wager Mr. Campbell had something to do with this; although, for the life of me, I don't know how or why."

"I do. It had to be Ellie. She can wrap her father around her little finger. But I can't go."

"Why not for heaven's sake?"

"I don't know how to dance. I'd feel like a fool."

Dancing classes in the cabin began that afternoon. The second day his mother said, "You are not a master, but you will not have to feel foolish. You can already dance better than some of the dandies. We used to be invited to the great house when your father was a captain, and there were always a few who protected the punch bowl, not being accomplished dancers and afraid of looking foolish. Avoid the punch bowl and you will do just fine. Now about your clothes."

She sized me up and smiled. "You asked me when your father died why we buried him in his oldest work clothes. Now you will see why. We are going to unpack the trunk and try his best clothes on. They should fit you fine. I will take them in a little if they need it.”

She was right, of course.

“If you don’t look like a gentleman, no man at the dance will. Try on your father’s wig.”

I pulled the powdered wig over my hair.

“It makes you look older.”

“I don’t like it, and they are going out of style.”

“Wear it anyway. You look grand in it. Ladies there will have their eyes on you. It makes you look so much like your father, you must wear it for me.”

She was right again.

Ellie seemed captivated. She told me, “No Lord ever looked more handsome and noble than you do.”

Smitten by her in the stylish low cut French dress, I returned her compliment. “Nor any Great Lady any more beautiful than you.”

I’d never visited the great house before, let alone the lavish ballroom. I gazed around enchanted and noticed the admiring glances of several young ladies. It distressed me rather than pleased me, because I wasn’t the only one who observed the attention I received from the women, some who were several years older than Ellie.

She forestalled my ardent admirers, keeping me in her arms one dance after another. My dancing ability impressed her. "You must have been dancing since you were young. You dance very well." She said.

"You can thank my mother for that, she taught me. You dance divinely yourself, and that dress is lovely on you. You are the most beautiful woman here."

Her angst was quelled until her best friend, Caroline, had the temerity to ask if I would take one dance with her. "You don't mind do you Ellie?" She asked.

She smiled, bit her lip and lied to her former friend, "No I don't mind, but just one dance." She moved to the punch bowl as we swirled around the room. It was a glorious night, it was a wretched night, a night of admiration, a night of jealousy, a night of change, a night of awakening, a magical night of promise.

Winter brought a false sense of peace to Johnstown after the ball, even as the gods of war were about to be released in faraway Massachusetts. Spring approached, word came to the village about Patrick Henry of the Virginia Colony, and a speech he had made. It prophesied war, and called for resisting English oppression. Noting the belligerent British attitude, he mocked delegate's efforts for peace, and he had ended his speech with the words, "Give me liberty or give me death." It birthed many tavern discussions, several shouting matches and a few fist fights. Sides were solidifying. The rumbling grew louder, the earth trembled. We were about to jump into the abyss.

****

In Boston, General Gage received reports of growing mischief in the city, of people arrested for insulting soldiers or ignoring regulations, but the thing which concerned him the most was word that the colonists in the countryside were forming militias, drilling and preparing for combat. He discussed the situation with his officers, and decided defusing the threat by confiscating guns and the stores of powder in Lexington and Concord would be the best course of action. The longer they waited the more prepared the rebels would become.

Gates' plan was supposed to be secret, but with so many soldiers, the word leaked out like juice through a sieve. The city contained men who were ready to ride and warn the countryside the British were coming. They lacked only the date and the hour.

April 18, 1775, a week before Ellie's 15th birthday, about 700 British soldiers prepared to march that night and be at Lexington in the early morning of April 19th. The militia that became known as Minutemen, had been forewarned by riders sent out by Joseph Warren who had learned the final piece of the puzzle just the day before.

At dawn, drums rumbling, the 700 professional soldiers marched onto the Lexington Green and halted, facing 77 terrified but determined militiamen. Both sides were ordered not to fire. A British Major yelled at the militia, "Throw down your arms! Ye villains, ye rebels!"

The commander of the militia, overawed by the huge force facing them, had just given the order for his men to disperse, when a shot rang out. The rumble of discontent erupted in a roar of British muskets, as they fired several volleys, killing 8 and wounding 9. The British suffered one slightly wounded.

They searched for weapons before continuing their march to Concord, where they expected to find a large store of arms. They were disappointed. The guns were already in the hands of the rebels, and over 400 of them confronted the British troops, who began their march back to Boston after a short skirmish at the bridge. A growing force of rebels dogged the British column, and fired on them from cover all the way back to Boston.

The army lost fewer than 100 soldiers, but the word went out, the vaunted British Army had been confronted and put to flight by a rag tag group of citizen soldiers. The boost to the American's morale was immediate, news of the battle spread like wild fire, and war became inevitable.

Chapter 8

Rebellion

The cold wind subsided, water dripped from bare tree limbs. The dark sky threatened more rain to come, but it could not quell the commotion. Men struggled through sticky mud up to their ankles in places. A crowd gathered in and around the inn. They pushed and shoved their way into the already packed tavern until it could hold no more.

A fur buyer from Boston had arrived at the inn bearing astounding news of events taking place in Massachusetts. He related a tale of death and destruction to all of us within earshot. Men outside heard the gruesome details second hand. The descriptions of how the colonists made the British pay in blood raised cheers and shouts, rending the air in raucous waves. All day, men retold the story, embellished it, and told it again. The event morphed into a huge battle with hundreds of British casualties.

I heard bits and pieces, enough to get a picture of what had taken place. The British soldiers killed militiamen. The survivors repelled the redcoats, sending them fleeing to Boston with heavy casualties. I concluded that was it in a nut shell.

I observed William standing, grim-faced at the edge of the crowd. He watched who cheered and who did not. I made no attempt to get closer or catch his attention.

When he mounted his horse and left, I moved to where I could watch him ride away. Several other men watched him going out of sight. I overheard one of them say, "Sure, there's one man who takes no pleasure in the kings soldiers being slapped down."

Another said, "Aye, that's true enough. He will bear closer watching by the safety committee that one will."

Another agreed, "I know, and there are a lot more like him. Most of the Scotch tenants on Sir John's land are King's men; quite a few of them served in the army. You won't see them cheering today."

In our village, the gulf widened between men who held the king in the highest regard, and the disenchanted. The irritating rift ruptured because of Lexington, leaving men to decide which side of the chasm were they on. Men of both persuasions streamed away from the tumult to spread the news.

I headed home, and burst through the door, nearly knocking it off the hinges. "Mother, Massachusetts is in rebellion. Soldiers killed many colonists, and then the redcoats were attacked and driven back to Boston. People are saying it means war."

"Hold on, where did you hear this? Were you working at Mr. Campbell's? Did you hear it from him?"

"No. It was too wet and sloppy for the oxen to work today. I walked over to see Ellie instead. I met a man on the way who asked me if I had heard the news. Before I could ask him what news, he grabbed my jacket and pulled me along to the inn. A man there told everyone, the people of Massachusetts have rebelled against the King"

"Calm down," she said, "and tell me exactly what you heard."

I pulled a chair up near mother, and told her everything I had been able to hear.

"That sounds serious, but how long has it been since the army shot those poor men for throwing snowballs at them? Five years I think. And the tea thrown into Boston Harbor? Talk of war surfaced after both of them. This may blow over as well. We will see."

"I've been thinking about joining the militia. What do you think? Should I?"

"I think you can make up your own mind about that. I admit I would prefer you not become a soldier, but you have my blessing no matter what you decide. I have heard every able bodied man 16 and older may be required to join. You may not have a choice."

In the end, we did nothing except wait to see what would come of the events, and what Sir John would do, if anything. Everyone knew the Johnson's loyalties lay with the crown, but he still commanded a great deal of respect. We didn't have to wait long for their response, or at least the response of Guy Johnson.

Colonel Guy Johnson traveled around our county haranguing groups in many communities. He always began his lecture with, "Hear me, ye would be rebels. Do not be misled by the recent events in the Massachusetts Colony. Not only were they exaggerated and mostly untrue, but it is only a matter of time until His Majesty's forces put down the rebellion and jail the instigators."

It was little wonder the result of his bellicose words was resentment and even disrespect from his audience. He appeared frustrated or angered by the resistance he received at every turn, and not long after, he left for Canada with about 150 people who believed as he did. The recently formed Tryon County Committee of Safety took Guy's departure in stride, but its members maintained a suspicious vigil over numerous men they considered Tories or Loyalists.

Sir John fell into that category, but the committee was conflicted about him. He remained at Johnson Hall with his wife and two daughters, and continued on with his job as the British Superintendent of Indian Affairs.

He attempted to navigate a difficult course, trying to preserve a friendly relationship with his neighbors and remaining tenants, while encouraging Loyalists to maintain a low profile and avoid arguments. For a while, things seemed to settle down on the surface, but everyone knew problems brewed throughout the colonies.

Chapter 9

Rebel or Tory

The lake effect snow pulled the spruce bows into steep curves, and deep drifts covered the ground. It was beautiful in its own way, but I puffed frosty clouds into the air, nearing Ellie's home exhausted from the arduous trek. Mr. Campbell sent me a message the day before and asked me to come because he wished to discuss something with me. I never ignored such a request, nor the opportunity to see Ellie.

I propped my snowshoes in a drift, and knocked on the door. Ellie opened it. "Come in Jacob. You will freeze to death out there." She held out a pair of slippers. "I watched for you. I knew you would come." She said.

I closed the door, took off my coat, sat down and exchanged my boots for the slippers. I looked around, and seeing no one, I kissed her. I swear my heart skipped a beat or two; the rounded tops of her breasts were only semi-hidden beneath a shawl. A large petticoat expanded the bottom of her dress and peeked through the small opening down the front. He could not imagine anyone more lovely than Ellie.

She said, "Come into the library. Father is waiting for you. He expected you would come as soon as you could." I saw the wink when she said, "I wonder whatever gave him that idea?"

I took her arm. I could hear and feel the rustling dress and petticoat, but resisted taking another glance at her breasts. "You certainly are all dressed up this morning."

"I'd always dress up for you." She replied.

William looked up from the papers on his desk. "Come in my boy," he said. "Thank you for coming. I know it is not a pleasant day."

"On the contrary, sir, it is a beautiful day, quiet and peaceful. Just a bit colder than I care for."

"He asked, "Would you like a cup of hot tea? You must be chilly."

"I would enjoy that, sir. It's very kind of you to ask."

He turned to his daughter. "Would you be a good girl and fetch us some tea?"

After she left, he turned his attention back to me. "She's a fine lass. A wee bit headstrong and a little wild. It's the Campbell in her, but she has her mother's looks. It seems to me the two of you have been seeing each other quite often."

"Is that why you asked me here, sir? We've done nothing improper, but I do like her very much."

"No, that's not why I asked you to come, but I'd have to be a fool or blind not to see how much she cares for you. Tell me, why did you join the militia?"

"I felt I had to obey the law."

"I thought so, but I have something I need to ask you. I want you to agree not to share it with others."

"If it's necessary, of course I agree."

"Good. Sir John wrote to Governor Tryon, informing him that he could raise at least 500 men to retake the forts the rebels have occupied, and put them to flight if the governor agreed. He is waiting even now for a reply."

"Is that why he stayed instead of leaving? Everyone expected he would follow Guy to Canada. It seems the committee of safety may be right to be suspicious of him.

"Ah yes, the committee. Did you know they are worried about me as well, because of my connections with Sir John?"

"But if he plans to raise men to resist the rebels, it would seem he will be in conflict with the committee."

"I believe he only wants to see peace return to New York, and I feel it is the right course of action. I have volunteered to join his force, and I'd like you to volunteer also. What do you say?"

"What does he say to what?" Ellie asked, returning with the tea.

"It's none of your affair, but I've asked him to join Sir John in his efforts to stop the rebellion before it gets any more serious, and more people get hurt. It's the only course of action that makes any sense. Parliament and the King will seek a peaceful solution to the rebel grievances if they will put lay down their arms."

"What do you say, Jacob, are you with us?"

Ellie butted in, "What do you mean it's none of my affair. If it concerns Jacob, it concerns me."

Her outburst drew a stern look from her father, but I smiled. "Sir, this is quite sudden, and I cannot give you an answer at this moment. Perhaps Sir John is right, I need time to think about it, but I will not betray your confidence."

"How long do you need?" He asked. "Actions may well begin in just a few days depending on the governor's reply."

"I will give you my answer on Wednesday. Thank you for the tea, but now I believe it would be best for me to leave. I assure you I will think carefully about what you said. Good day to you, Sir."

Ellie followed me to the door. "You could stay for a little while with me in the parlor. Father would not mind."

"I am truly tempted to stay, but I feel I should go." I took her hand, kissed it, and promised, "I will see you in two days."

"She sighed. "I'll be waiting for you."

Chapter 10

The Meeting

I knew what I had to do before I left the Campbell's two days earlier, but I wanted the extra time to rethink it. I wanted my answer to be respectful. I didn't want to offend Ellie's father, so I ran through a number of variations. Wednesday morning came all too soon.

I loathed leaving the cabin. It was so cold; the trees had been popping all night. The sub -zero temperature burned my face when I took care of the animals in the morning. I made breakfast last as long as I could, but I had made a promise. So after lunch, I bundled up, wrapped a wool scarf around my neck and face and stepped into snowshoes. I didn't relish the cold weather or the cold reception I expected to get from William when I gave him my decision.

Ellie had watched for me, and opened the door before I knocked. "Oh Jacob, I hoped you would come, but I was afraid you wouldn't. Father told me it was foolish of me to sit all day by the window waiting for you."

"I told him I would be back in two days, and I always try to keep my promises."

"He would not have been disappointed if you hadn't come. I think he will be surprised to see you." She said.

I observed the plain outfit she wore and knew she really had not expected me either.

"Would you let him know I'm here, Ellie?"

She dropped the slippers for me and went to tell her father. I heard muted conversation from the library, but could not make out their words. When Ellie came back, she said, "He wants you to come right in."

A fire blazed and crackled in the fireplace, and I was truly thankful for the heat. The room was so cheerful and inviting, I felt guilty as I looked at the smile on William's face.

He welcomed me in. "Come in, my man. I didn't think you would brave such cold. I am impressed."

"I promised I would come."

I sensed Ellie had left and glanced to see.

"She will be back in a minute. Have a seat."

Ellie returned and with her mother. "My goodness, Jacob, did my daughter lure you out on a day like this?"

I liked Mrs. Campbell. Ruth was tall and slender, with a beautiful smile, and I believed she was on my side where Ellie and I were concerned. It was not as easy to read her father, but he had never tried to discourage them.

"I cannot blame Ellie for my venturing forth on such an inclement day. I told your husband two days ago that I would come and talk with him. But in truth, I would have come if only she alone had asked me."

Ruth looked at Ellie and then at her husband and nodded her head toward her daughter.

He said, "This has nothing to do with Ellie. As you know, Sir John is raising men, and I asked Jacob to join us. He vowed to return today with his answer."

"It's good to see you anyway, Jacob. I brought you both some scones to go with your tea."

She turned to go. "Elspeth, come to the kitchen with me and let the men talk."

Ellie glanced at me as she slipped out the door and reluctantly closed it. She saw there was no longer a smile on my face, and my head bowed slightly.

William picked up one of the scones, still warm from the heat of the oven. "Try one of these scones. They are my favorite, raspberry. They are wonderful."

"I'm sure they are, sir. Not even my mother makes better."

"So tell me Jacob, have you decided to join us?" He asked.

"Sir, I was honored that you asked me, and that you trusted me, and I know you mean well, but I have my mother who needs someone to help her, and would prefer I stay home."

"I take it your answer is no." He paused looking thoughtfully at me. "Well Jacob, I don't think any less of you for your decision, and I'm sure Ellie will be relieved, but I think you are turning your back on a great opportunity. Are you sure you do not wish to join us?" He asked.

"Yes, quite sure."

"Then let's say no more about it. Eat your scone. Actually Ellie made them, not the Mrs. There is some butter on the tray if you would like some.

Chapter 11

Disappointment and Decisions

Governor Tryon's answer came on January 20. A force of Continental troops under the command of General Schuyler, along with a large number of Tryon County Militia, arrived and confiscated Sir John's arms and those of 300 followers. Beneath his calm exterior, he probably seethed, but any resistance at that point would have been futile and dangerous.

I rode over to see Ellie after hearing about the guns. The snow settled and it was an easy journey for the horse, besides it was time he got some exercise. Surprised, she invited me in. "Are you here because of what happened? If you are, father is not home."

"No, I came over to see you, but I did want to talk your father also. They took his gun?"

"Yes, and he is outraged."

"I can understand that. I think I would be upset too if it happened to me. But I wanted to talk about us, not that. We have talked a lot about our future, but I've never proposed to you. Will you marry me?"

"You know I will. I would have married you last year when I was 15 if you had asked. But you need to ask my father for his approval.

I had disappointed Ellie's father when I declined to join the men who wanted to restore order as they saw it. He made light of it at the time, but after the governor sent soldiers, a not-so-subtle change occurred in our relationship. I had been comfortable in their home, but now I felt awkward. Ellie said I imagined things, but there was a chill in the air that had nothing to do with the weather

After that, she clung to me, keeping me out of his presence as much as possible. When we did meet, he was cordial, but distant, and he made little effort to engage me in conversation.

"I'm telling you, Ellie, your father is not pleased seeing us together. You must see that."

She pulled me closer. "Nonsense. He struggled with what the governor did; it has nothing to do with us."

"It has everything to do with us. It's written in the expression on his face. It colors everything he says and does. He keeps to himself as much as possible, and your mother doesn't join us in the parlor anymore. He probably discouraged her.

"Now, there you are wrong. You told me not to say anything about your asking me to marry you, but I had to tell mother, and I asked her not to tell father until you talked to him. I don't need a chaperone anymore, that's all."

I was almost persuaded as she kissed me, and pressed her body into mine. "When are you going to ask him? I'm 16 and soon I'll be 17. I don't want to wait, but you have to ask him."

"I'm only waiting for the right moment. He is so preoccupied, sometimes he doesn't even hear what I say, and probably doesn't care."

"Well, I've been patient, but I don't want to wait forever. I want to set a date for our wedding," She slipped her right hand behind my head and ran her fingers through my hair.

She was right. My body ached for her each time we were together. I needed to talk to her father, and we needed to set a date. "I promise I will ask your father when I have finished planting. We can be married on Saturday, June first. Would that be acceptable?"

"Why wait so long to ask him?"

"I want to put as much time as possible between what happened and when I ask. Things will be better then.

****

Sir John bided his time, and the crisis subsided sufficiently for the governor to relent and pardon him, providing he agreed not to repeat his actions, but the guns would not be returned. That probably was an unwise decision on the governor's part, because Sir John and his men were not about to forgive and forget the seizure of their guns. I could understand, they were private property and needed for hunting and protection. Not retuning them was an insult and a hardship for the men.

Some men had had enough and left for Canada soon after the offense. Others, including William Campbell, remained with Sir John, still hoping what they saw as sanity, would return. It was in those confusing days that I saw George once more. He returned to Blessed Hope on February 6, and the day after arriving, he stopped by our home.

I was excited to see him. "Come in, George, what brings you back to us?"

"Father asked me to come home. He had some important things to share with me. I got home just yesterday, but I wanted so much to see you and your mother."

"I appreciate that. What's going on that he wanted you to come home? Is it about the guns?"

"That's part of it. He is very concerned about the state of affairs. You know how he feels about the rebellion and how those who are loyal to the King are being treated badly by the governor. Friends and neighbors are turning against him too. He is bitter. He told me, 'The people who proclaim liberty so brazenly are reluctant to grant it to us.' He has even considered leaving for Canada. He told me if Sir John leaves, he will go with him."

"I didn't know that he was thinking about leaving. The committee will take his property if he goes to Canada."

"I know I can speak freely with you, you are a true friend. You have not turned your back on my family. Father is concerned about what would happen to his property if he should leave. That's why he asked me to come. He wanted to know if I would go with them if he left."

"What did you tell him? Would you go?"

"No, I told him I would stay in Hartford; I didn't want to give up my position with the solicitor. I had worked too hard for it"

"Was he upset with you?"

"He told me he had expected it, and that was why he needed to see me. He wanted to know if there was any way to avoid losing Blessed Hope. I told him he could stay here and endure the abuse of the neighbors. That didn't seem to set well with him, and he asked if there was any other way?"

"Did you have another solution?"

"I told him he could sell to someone and try to buy it back later. I could draw up a legal contract for that. Now he wants me to buy Blessed Hope, and if they should leave, it would be mine all nice and legal. The government couldn't seize it."

"Are you going to do it?"

"Yes. He is going to basically sign it over to me for a small down payment, but I had to agree to two conditions. One was that when the rebellion was over, the rest of the family could come back to live there. The second was that I had to promise I would not join the militia."

"And you agreed?"

"Of course. What else could I do? It would become mine when he dies anyway. It would have been foolish to ignore the alternative."

"I guess you are right. How long are you going to be here?"

"I'm leaving day after tomorrow unless there is a storm."

"Then let's sit down and have a spot of tea, and you can tell me all about your studies and your work. It must be interesting."

"Sometimes, but most of the time it's boring. Deeds, wills, transactions, and law suits are all part of my world now, but I've come to like it."

We spent the afternoon enjoying each other's company, and sharing what we had been doing. When he was getting ready to leave he asked me, "Is there any other news you haven't told me?"

"Not that I can think of."

"You realize I've talked with Ellie?"

"If she said I asked her to marry me, it's true, but I haven't asked your father for his permission yet. I told Ellie I will, but not until things quiet down a bit."

"Well Jacob, if you remember, I did tell you I would make a great brother-in-law. I'm looking forward to it. Be sure to keep me posted "

When he left for Connecticut, all was well with the family, but all was not well on the political front.

Chapter 12

Planning For Life

Things changed after George left. I picked Ellie up at least twice a week to come and visit us. She had been to our home a few times before; it took on a new meaning now. I quit worrying about what her father thought of me. As long as Ellie loved me and agreed to marry me. What could go wrong?

I admit I felt relieved that we had a date set, and mother loved the change. She told Ellie.

"You don't know it, but I've loved you from the first day I met you."

Ellie blushed and gave her a hug. She helped mother with cooking and chores around the house. It was a happy arrangement. I went to pick her up one morning and she gave me a kiss and invited me in.

"My parents are at Sir John's. We finally have a chance to be alone. Let's sit in the parlor."

She brought in some tea and cuddled with me. She bubbled over with ideas about our future.

"Where will we live when we are married? We could live here for a while, but I think it would be better if we lived at your home. What do you think?"

"I believe my mother would be overjoyed. You have seen how much she enjoys it when you visit."

"Then we could live there, but I think we need more room. We could build a bigger house, or we could add onto yours."

"I think building would be easier than adding on, but why do we need so much room?"

"Well, first of all, we need a bedroom of our own. We can't very well sleep in your kitchen."

"I'm sure I could add a small bedroom to the cabin."

"I was thinking of something more than that."

"Why would we need more than that?"

"For the children of course, silly. It could get quite crowded with four or five little ones running around."

"By the time you get done, we will need a house as large as Blessed Hope."

"Exactly. I would love a home just like that, and we would have a room for Martha."

"I don't think we can build that right away. I'm afraid we will have to make do with the cabin for a while."

"Well, maybe before the babies start coming?"

"We will see when that time comes."

"Just think of it, Jacob, three handsome boys and two beautiful girls. The boys will help you on the farm, and I'll teach the girls to cook. The boys will become doctors or lawyers or officers, and the girls will marry handsome, wealthy, gentlemen."

"How long have you been planning all of this?

"Since I turned 14. I told mother I was going to marry you. I was thinking when I turned 15, but you didn't ask me then."

It sounds like you've got the family all figured out."

"Not just that. With all the help you'll have, you could buy more land, plant more wheat, raise sheep and horses, and have a big flock of chickens."

It sounded like I was going to be one busy man in more ways than one.

****

The April sun defeated the snow and warmed the soil. Spring winds wicked the moisture from the ground, and I planted oats on April 6 and 7. Ellie joined me as I sowed. "If you get all the oats in, why are you waiting until May to plant your corn?"

She might become a farmer's wife, but she had a lot to learn about farming. "The ground has to be drier and warmer, and we may still get frosts before May 10. If I plant too early, the corn will not sprout, it will rot in the ground instead, or if it does come up, a late frost could kill it, and I would have to start all over."

"Then why are you planting oats?"

"They don't mind the cold; they actually grow better when it is cool, and a bit of frost will not kill them.

My oats were still swelling in the ground, and it was a beautiful day when I visited Ellie. She was outside cleaning small branches and leaves out of the flower beds. The daffodils were up several inches, but there were no buds yet. She saw me and came running. "I'm so glad you came today. You probably will not believe this, but Simon was here yesterday and asked father if he could court me."

"What was his answer?"

"He told him it was up to me, that I had a mind of my own."

"And?"

"I told him I was not interested, that I was already spoken for."

"As you are, but watch out for him. He may not take no for an answer. I don't trust him. He is an evil man.

Chapter 13

THE SURPRISE

William relented in April. He spoke to me about a number of things, but never about the affront suffered. He smiled any time he came upon Ellie and me. On the surface, it appeared everything had smoothed out, but everyone seemed edgy. The long suffering Tories were subjected to increasing insults and obvious distain, born of the suspicion and anger of their neighbors. I myself, questioned how long Sir John could maintain his position in Tryon County and marveled at how steadfast his supporters remained.

May was so glorious. I completed most of my planting before mid-month, but I still found time for Ellie and me each day. She ran out of patience waiting for me. "You must ask my father. You said you would right after planting."

She pressed herself against me, kissing me deeply and forced me back on the ground. "Don't you feel what I do? Don't tell me no, your body is betraying you right now."

"Yes, I feel as you do. Do you think I am made out of stone?"

She giggled, "Sometimes it feels like you are."

I wanted her more than I had ever wanted anything else in my life. "I will ask your father on Monday. Even a saucy little thing like you can wait that long if I can."

She gave me a hug that left me breathless. "It will be the longest three days of my life. Do you promise? Monday?"

"Of course I promise. I want you with every ounce of my body, but I want you as my wife."

"I could be your wife right now."

"I don't want to do anything that would jeopardize the relationship with your parents. We will wait."

Sunday morning, she came and sat in the pew with me and my mother. She whispered, "Father is very distraught. We nearly did not come to church. He is furious and insists that you come to see him this afternoon."

"Do you know what he wants?"

"Yes, but I can't speak of it here."

I could not keep my thoughts on the pastor's sermon. My mind conjured up several different scenarios, none of them good. It didn't help as we parted after church, she said, "Please come as quickly as you can. It's important."

I took mother home and ate a slice of bread and drank a cup of tea before leaving to see Mr. Campbell. I walked instead of saddling the horse. I dreaded the unknown, nearly oblivious of the world around me as I hurried along. In my mental fog, I nearly ran into Simon Tarbell on the road before I saw him.

I'm sorry, Simon."

He growled back, "You will be."

I had no idea of what he meant by that, but Simon Tarbell was an evil tempered bully, and he had little use for me. I knew it was best if I just kept walking and ignored his remark. There was nothing to be gained by stirring him up.

"Go ahead. Walk away!" He shouted after me.

I left him and his unpleasantness behind me, and arrived at the Campbell's, welcomed by daffodils dancing in the light breeze. They lined both sides of a perfectly level slate walk leading to a red door. The words "BLESSED HOPE," were carved in the sturdy lintel above the door. Ellie's mother chose the name when the home was built, and my father had carved it.

I raised my hand to knock, but Ellie opened the door first, her hand reaching out for mine. I lifted it to my lips and kissed it. "I came as soon as I could. What is going on? Is your father angry with me? With us?"

"No, nothing like that. Sir John received a warning last night. General Schuyler is on his way from Albany with a large number of soldiers and militia to arrest him. Even at this moment, he is preparing to leave before they can get here, and many of those loyal to the King will be leaving with him. We are going too."

"What about your home? You must know the property of Tories who leave for Canada is being confiscated."

"Father has taken care of that. I hadn't told you, but he sold our home to George in February. He had to agree he would never join the militia. It was all very legal and proper."

I didn't reveal I already knew. "So why did your father want me to come today?"

"He is in the Library, you should ask him."

Papers flew into the fireplace blazing up before curling and turning black. He reached to pick up another handful when he saw me. "Come in, Jacob, thank you for coming so quickly. I have something I need to ask you. It's not for others to know, but we are going to Canada. Will you come with us?"

I did not want to upset him, but I had to be honest. "Ellie already told me that, sir, but I cannot go with you.

My place is here with my mother; the safety committee might take her home."

"I see. Have I misjudged you? Will you go and inform the authorities?"

"No sir, I will not, but you can be sure they will learn soon enough."

"Sit down, Jacob. Listen to me. There is a war coming, it has already started, and I would prefer to be on the winning side with my king. Do you actually think the rebels can win against the power of England? They have no chance, but when war comes here it will be friend against friend, neighbor against neighbor, and there will be no mercy. You have seen how people are treating one another already. Do you want to face that?

"I am a farmer, sir, not a soldier."

"You think farmers will be safe? Were they safe when we fought the French and their Indians? Farmers will be the first targets for the savages."

"I still cannot go, sir," I said. "

Gathering up my courage while there might still be a chance, I asked, "Would you give me your daughter's hand in marriage?"

He scowled, looking at his daughter and then back to me. "No, she will not marry you. She will go to Canada with us where she will be safe." Sighing, he added, "I think you should go now. Remember, say nothing."

Ellie walked me to the door, pleading, "Please Jacob, come with us. I know father will agree to our marriage if you come."

"Ellie, I love you. Can't you see, you can stay here with me? You could even leave with me now. He can't force you to go."

"I can't. I have to go with them. If you really love me, you would go too."

"I do love you, but I can't go," I said, dropping her hand and turning.

'Wait, before you go there is something in the barn I need to show you. I have had it hidden for some time, but I now I want you to have it."

I followed her to the barn where she told me it was in the hay mow. "Go ahead of me and I'll follow you up. I'm sure you will be surprised."

Scene 14

ELLIE'S GONE

My life changed in the hay mow. Neither of us would ever be completely the same again. I gently picked hay out of her hair. I groped for words. I couldn't say I was sorry, because I wasn't, and after all, it was her idea. Telling her I loved her seemed too shallow. Finally I told her, I wished the day could never end.

"Does that mean you will come with us to Canada?"

I heard the hope in her voice. It tore me up, but I told her it was not possible. "I don't want to lose you, but I could never be happy in Canada, my place is here, but I do love you."

My chest ached, and the daffodils seemed to be waving goodbye, as I walked away from the sounds of her crying. I had risen to the heights only to fall into the depths of despair.

I had not gotten to the village, when my way was blocked by three men, one of them holding a cudgel, Simon Tarbell. The other two were men whom I had thought of as friends, but their faces were dark, distorted, and threatening. "Step aside." I said.

"Are you going to make us?" Said Tarbell with a sinister smile. "We know where you've been, plotting with that tory, Campbell. You've been having your way with his slutty daughter as well."

Moving to stand directly in front of Simon with my fists clenched, I said. "Move out of my way or I'll take that club out of your hand and use it on the three of you. Henry and John, I don't know what has gotten into you two, but back off or I swear I will make you wish you had."

They stepped back to the edge of the road. "Simon said you were plotting with Campbell burn our homes and kill us all." They explained.

Tarbell's support evaporated. Slowly he stepped back, "We will let you go this time, but you haven't heard the last of this."

Moving closer to Simon, I said, "Say what you want about me, but know this, if you ever speak of Ellie that way again, you will need more than a club and friends. I will not let you off as easy as I did last time. I will beat you to within an inch of your life. Do you understand me? Now get out of my way."

He said nothing but took a couple steps backward off the road.

Three days later the citizens of Tryon County were coming to the realization that a great change had taken place. Sir John vanished along with many of his supporters. By July we heard that he was raising a volunteer regiment of loyalist in Canada called the king's Royal Yorkers. A substantial number of the recruits had been our neighbors. William Campbell had been appointed a Captain in the new unit. No one knew what was going to happen, but no one would have predicted the savage war that would soon envelope the North Country and ravage Tryon County.

Suspicious eyes burned into me, watching for any false move. My earlier relationship with the Campbell's branded me as a potential Tory, so June first I joined the Third Regiment of the Tryon County Militia as a private to allay their fears. I would have joined the Continental Army, but I did not want to leave my mother alone

I was still mourning my loss when George came back to Blessed Hope, gave me a copy of his deed, and asked me if I would watch over his property for him, and I could farm it in payment for my services. He was striking in his new Lieutenant's uniform. He had joined the Connecticut Line of the Continental Army. He explained, "I only promised father not to join the militia, and I didn't."

He also brought a letter for me from Ellie. I wondered how that could be, but George told me he had a relative in New York City who could get mail in and sometimes out. He left the next day, and I gave him a letter to send to her. It was the last correspondence I had with her during the war, and I couldn't be sure she got it.

In July we received news of the Declaration of Independence. We were a nation, at least on paper, but no one believed we would get off without a fight. There was hope that the Iroquois would join us or at least remain neutral, but negotiations with the Indians fell short of that goal. The nearest tribe, The Oneida, refused to assist the British, and remained neutral in the conflict; although, more than a few actually served our cause in one way or another. The Tuscarora were nominally neutral, but the Mohawk, Onondaga, Seneca, and Cayuga served as fierce irregulars with the British.

There were a few minor raids in 1776, but on the whole, the threat of Iroquois attacks and large raids from Canada never materialized. It began to look like we would be spared in the conflict. That later proved to be a vain hope.

In October, a deserter from the Royal Yorkers returned to our village. He swore allegiance to our new country, and was allowed to remain among us. He brought news about a number of people from our area, including Ellie. She had married an Ensign in the Royal Yorkers. The news devastated me. I tried to forget her by farming longer hours and training with the militia, but she was always there.

It was in the militia that I fell in with Ananias Archer, a fellow private in our regiment. He was a few years older than I, and had a wife and a baby daughter. He joined the militia in 1775 to protect his family if Tryon County were attacked.

I didn't know how fortunate I was to have him as a friend, and what a large part he would play in my life. He didn't live all that far away from us, but for some reason, our paths had seldom crossed, and before the militia I really didn't know him. He was rugged, broad shouldered, and exuded confidence. With his abilities, he should have been at least a sergeant or even an officer, but as fate would have it, he became my mentor and my best friend.

They didn't teach us in the militia how to reload quickly or how to reload while running, but he showed me how to do both. I shared with him my fear that I might turn tail and run from battle. He didn't laugh at me.

He told me, "You will do fine when the time comes. There is a time to stand and fight and a time to run, and a wise man knows the difference. You can be frightened and still fight like a bear, but you can be as brave as a bear and still run like a rabbit when you must. If there is a fight, stay close to me. You will be fine."

Chapter 15

Dinner with Ananias

Reports of fighting around New York City and Long Island filtered into the North Country. The British maintained a strong grip on the City, with more troops arriving on a regular basis until they had General Washington's army outnumbered ten to one. General Washington and his men fought valiantly but the British forced him to retreat from one position after another. It seemed there was plenty of fighting going on, but it wasn't in Tryon County. Amazingly, Washington kept his dwindling force intact, but it looked like the only way he could save the army would be to evacuate his men to New Jersey.

News was always slow to arrive, but I received a short letter from George in October. He wrote:

> "I've been engaged in several battles, and our Continental soldiers have stood their ground well. We have given the red coats as good as we have gotten, but there are just too many of them. I hope to get a short leave, but I'm not sure just when that

might be. I have not heard anything from Ellie."

Some of our single men left to join the army, but most, like Ananias and me, remained in the North Country with the militia. I talked often about Ellie and how much I missed her. One afternoon, after drill, Ananias invited me to come to his home and meet his wife and daughter.

He stopped and opened the door. "Wait just a moment. I want to let Elizabeth know we are here. She's expecting you to be with me, but I want to make sure she is ready for us."

Reappearing a few moments later, he said, "Come on in. Dinner is ready, and the baby is sleeping."

His wife was an attractive woman, and as it turned out, a great cook. She asked a lot of questions about me and my mother before her questions drifted in another direction.

"Ananias told me you were going to get married, but your lady ran off to Canada. I'm sorry for you. Have you been looking for someone to take her place?"

"No, ma'am, I really haven't given it much thought. I've been trying to forget her, but that has been hard, and the last I heard, she had gotten married in Canada."

"So she is not likely to be coming back?"

"Not likely, ma'am. She has a husband and a new life now."

"I apologize for bringing it up. I know it must hurt you, but if you ever decide to look for another young lady, let me know. I might be able to help you out."

The baby woke, and the conversation came to a close. Ananias held Amy up for me to see; she was beautiful. I held her for a few minutes before I left. I had never had a baby in my arms before, but she seemed to like me, and I didn't drop her.

Walking home that evening, I thought about what his wife had said. I hadn't even considered looking for someone to take Ellie's place, but her words started me thinking about what the future might hold, and if there might be another woman that could possibly fill the void Ellie had left.

The formerly invisible women became strikingly apparent in my eyes and my mind, but many of the fair maidens were spoken for or already married and I had no intention of sparking a girl who didn't appeal to me. I was interested in finding a wife, but I wasn't desperate, not yet.

Ananias and I discussed my dilemma as he helped me with haying. "You know, Elizabeth has someone in mind that she would like you to meet."

"I remember she said she might be able to help me out if I started looking for someone."

"She was referring to her younger sister, Penelope. She is slightly older than you and she is a real beauty."

"So why isn't she married?"

"If you will agree to come for dinner Friday and meet her, I will share her situation. Jacob, you must know I wouldn't do anything to displease you or hurt you. I consider you a valuable friend. What do you say?"

I felt a little fenced in, but on the other hand, it wouldn't hurt to meet his sister-in-law. I have to admit, I was curious about her.

"I agree. What is her situation?"

"She is very self-conscious and quite shy. When she was a young girl, she was hurt in an accident which permanently injured her left arm and shoulder. She only has limited use of that arm. She was teased because of it when she was growing up, and she is very sensitive about it."

"Well, that's nothing horrible. I thought maybe you were going to tell me she was a dwarf or had some sort of incurable disease."

He laughed. "She is a beautiful and very gentle person. She just hasn't met anyone yet who can see her for what she is beyond her handicap. You are still going to come, right?"

"Certainly. Your wife is a great cook and I'd be pleased to meet her sister."

CHAPTER 16

Penelope

How can I describe the first time I met Miss Penelope Jecocks? I arrived excited and expectant, but at the same time I was apprehensive and a bit queasy. I imagined her from beautiful with a barely noticeable problem with her left arm, to rather plain with a badly withered extremity. One might call our meeting a blind encounter.

Ananias introduced me, and I knew I had made the right decision. Her flawless visage dispelled any doubts, even though I noticed she stood turned slightly to her left.

"Won't you have a seat, Mr. Morrissey?" She pointed to the bench in a lilting voice.

She sat to my left, I to her right with a respectable space between us. My tongue tripped over itself, but I finally got it under control. "Your dress is lovely."

"Thank you, Mr. Morrissey. I made it myself."

"It does you credit. I've never seen better work."

"You flatter me, but thank you again. I understand you are a close neighbor."

"I'm about a 10 to 15 minute ride away depending on the weather and the horse. And where are you from?"

"Our father has a farm about twenty miles southeast of Johnstown."

We traded a few such pleasantries, but additional conversation did not come easily, and dinner came as a welcome relief. Elizabeth talked more than the other three of us combined, and the conversation was about the food, the baby, or tales from early life on the Jecocks' farm. I noticed Penelope seldom commented on what was being said, and a couple times she blushed, but she seemed to enjoy herself. Night finally caught us almost unaware, and I reluctantly bid them all a good night.

The quarter moon cast a tenuous light over the countryside, but my surefooted horse knew the way home without my guidance. Unhampered, I reflected on my visit as I rode. I found Penelope to be quiet, almost mysterious, and very easy on the eyes. I never noticed the condition of her arm, and being rocked by the gait of my mount, I realized her injury was unimportant, at least to me.

Ananias and I farmed the Campbell land together, and Saturday was just another workday. Our common labor produced a welcomed addition to both our incomes. We often talked about our crops, the weather, the militia and the war while we worked, but that morning I wanted to talk about Penelope.

"I had a wonderful time last night. Thank you for having me over. Will Penelope be staying with you long?"

"That's hard to say, but I believe she will be here for at least a week. Her father will come for her sometime after that."

"I thought I might invite her to go to church with mother and me tomorrow. Do you think she would like to go?"

"You will have to stop over and ask her yourself, but I think she would accept the invitation. She was impressed with your not trying to get a look at her bad arm, nor mentioning it. She told Elizabeth she hadn't been expecting such a handsome man, and she was pleasantly surprised when she saw you. Yes, sir, I'd say you have a good chance."

I felt a bit guilty about how quickly Ellie faded into a pleasant memory, and my thoughts of Penelope hurried the process along. I knew I at least wanted to get to know her better while I had the chance. Besides, Ellie had married shortly after she went to Canada; I was the one who had been betrayed.

When we finished our day's work, I accompanied Ananias home and asked if I could see Penelope. She came to the door, stepped outside and closed it.

"What can I do for you, Mr. Morrissey?"

"First of all, please call me Jacob. I would like to have you join my mother and me for church tomorrow morning."

"Jacob, you don't need to ask me just because my brother–in-law put you up to it."

"What? No, he didn't do any such thing."

"He told you about my arm, right?"

"Yes he did. He told me before I came last night. It didn't make any difference then, and it doesn't now."

"Are you so sure?" She reached out with her left arm. "Look at it."

I surprised her, taking her hand. The scar on her twisted forearm struck me, and her upper arm remained close to her side. "Ugly isn't it?" She asked.

"It looks like it must have been very painful, but it doesn't look ugly. It makes no difference to me in any case. I would still like you to come to church with us, if you are willing."

"If you are not just being kind to me because of my arm, then I would very much like to go."

"Then it's agreed. I'll come and get you in the morning. Tomorrow promises to be a clear day, and having you with us will make it even better." I tipped my cap. "Until then, Penelope."

She was the main topic of conversation at the table that night. I told mother about Penelope the night before, but those comments were rather rudimentary. Now, I couldn't say enough.

"Honestly mother, I was afraid that she might not want to come with us, but she agreed. She showed me her arm, like it would make me less interested in her. There is no reason for her to believe she is somehow less a woman, or less attractive because of her injury. You are going to love her."

"She sounds like a proper young lady. How old is she?"

"About a year older than I am."

"Is she anything like Ananias's wife? You've always held her in high regard."

"Yes, but she is even prettier, and more reserved and quiet. I like her."

"Are you thinking she might make you a good wife?"

"I haven't known her long enough to say. I would certainly like to get to know her better, and I wanted to see what you think of her."

"When you pick her up tomorrow, why don't you invite her to stay for dinner? That would give us a little time to know each other."

Chapter 17

Learning About Penelope

Elizabeth and her sister stood outside as I approached. Penelope wore a blue bonnet, a blue dress, and a grey shawl. She looked magnificent. I brought the wagon to a stop beside them, got down, and walked around to where they stood. "Good morning, Elizabeth, Miss Jecocks, I hope you haven't been standing outside for too long."

"Only for a few minutes before we saw you coming," Elizabeth said, "Pen wasn't able stand it to wait inside any longer."

I took Penelope's hand and walked her to the wagon. "Allow me to help you up."

She mounted the wagon effortlessly, and I took my place on the left side of the wagon seat beside her. "Are you all settled?"

"Yes, I'm ready." She turned and waved goodbye to her sister, and we were off.

"I'm sorry you have to ride in this wagon. It's pretty bumpy. We have a sleigh for winter, but we don't own a proper carriage."

"It's quite all right; my father doesn't have a carriage either. I'm practiced getting into a wagon and enduring the bumps."

"I can see that. I might also say you look very lovely this morning."

"Thank you. It's my sister's dress, but she insisted I wear it."

"I didn't mean the dress. I meant you."

She smiled and blushed. We rode in silence; just happy to be together. I know I was happy anyway.

We picked up mother, and I hardly had to take any part in the conversation. The two of them talked like old friends; I don't know how they found so much to visit about. With three of us on the seat, Penelope had no choice but to rest against me as we rode. Her leg rubbed against mine—more than it had to, it seemed—of course I didn't mind.

Several men looked her up and down approvingly. She was a new face, an attractive one, and I couldn't fault them for noticing. She took my arm, and we walked in and found our seats. She sat between me and mother and part way through the short service, I felt her arm cross mine to work our hands together. I only glanced at her, but I completely lost track of the pastor's words.

I had forgotten to ask her to stay with us for dinner until we were halfway home. "Miss Jecocks, Mother and I were hoping you would have dinner with us before I take you back to your sister."

"Why thank you, Jacob. I would be delighted."

She helped mother get dinner on the table and with the cleanup. Her willingness to help, even though she was a guest, made a good impression on Mother. Putting the last of the dishes away, Mother took a small box from the shelf and placed it on the table. "Do you play dominos, Miss Jecocks?"

"Oh yes. My father loves the game. We even let him win at times."

"Well it is the Sabbath, but I don't believe the Lord will hold a bit of merriment against us." She said, spilling the dominos out of the box onto the table. "Have a seat, and we will see just how good you are."

The love and laughter around the table portended a new and different life for each of us. Penelope had a soft side, but she was also a competitor. She and Mother enjoyed themselves immensely, they were worthy adversaries; it felt like I was just along for the ride.

Tea time came as a gracious break for me. I don't really like to lose either, but sadly I would be taking her home soon.

The short trip back to Ananias's home differed from the morning. She talked freely, sharing her feelings, comments, and questions.

"Your mother is a wonderful lady and a great cook. I hope I will be able to cook even half as well as she does when I have a husband."

"Do you like cooking?"

"Of course I do, but I feel I still have things to learn."

"Don't we all? You will do just fine. Any man would be a fool not to let you practice on him."

"Elizabeth tells me you and Ananias work another farm in addition to your own. That must keep you terribly busy."

"Your brother-in-law is a hard worker and a great partner. We work well together, and yes, the extra land stretches us, but it also makes it possible for us to provide better for our families."

"Jacob, tell me about Ellie."

Caught unaware, I asked, "What do you want to know?"

"What was she like?"

"She was beautiful, dainty, well educated, and made great scones. She was always there for me. She was fun to be around, and from the time she was twelve, she had her cap set for me."

"Did you love her?"

"Yes, very much. We were going to be married, but she chose to go to Canada with her parents even though I begged her to stay."

"Do you still love her?"

Conflicted, I searched for the answer. She had left me. She had married another man. She would never be mine, but had I ever stopped loving her?"

I sighed, "I suppose in a way I still do. I probably will always have a place for her in my heart, but it will be different from what we once shared. I can forgive her, but she is gone, and I want to move on with my life as she has already done."

"Are you thinking about anyone else?"

"Maybe. I'm not sure."

"Maybe? Don't take too long making up your mind. You are in the militia. You could be called out tomorrow to find and attack a raiding party and possibly be killed. None of us knows if we will see next week or be gone. My advice is, live for today; tomorrow may never come."

The ride turned silent, thoughts swirling around my head. I knew we were dancing around our relationship, each knowing what we wanted, but neither of us willing to approach it head-on even as I wished her goodnight at the cabin.

Chapter 18

Mohawk Raiders

The morning sun hadn't yet raised the temperature in our cabin, and I was about to get up and start a fire, when an insistent knocking rattled our door and brought me out of bed wide awake. I slipped on my pants and opened the door.

"The militia is being called out. There is a Mohawk raiding party on the way south from Oswegatchie. An Oneida brave saw them and came with the warning. Get to town as quickly as you can." The messenger left as quickly as he came, on his way once more.

The thought struck me that Penelope must be some sort of prophet. She had told me I could be "called out tomorrow," and tomorrow was here. I hoped she was not accurate about my possibly being killed. I told Mother where I headed off to, grabbed some parched corn, picked up my powder horn, shot bag, and my gun. My heart pounded in my chest in anticipation of a possible battle.

I fell in with the disjointed group of armed militiamen milling around on the parade grounds. Rampant talk and speculation tittered through the crowd. There had not been enough time for all of our regiment to arrive, but the Colonel quieted us down and began to inform us what was taking place.

"Men, this is not a drill, there are warriors on their way. The Oneida who brought the news said they were following the Indian trail from Oswegatchie, so we know about where we should be able to intercept them. The report indicated there were about 12 Indians in the group, but it could be an advance party. I would like 30 single men to volunteer to scout them out and destroy them if possible. We can't use more. Too many of us might alert them. Everyone else should keep a close watch at home with your gun always nearby."

There were twice as many volunteers as the colonel had asked for, but Lieutenant Forsythe selected thirty of us including me. By midday we had our instructions, and we were joined by three Oneidas who would scout for us.

We estimated the raiding party to be about halfway to our valley, about 65 to 70 miles away. Night found us bedding down about 15 miles north of our families. We expected we would probably locate them in about three days, and set an ambush for them, but three days later we found no sign of them.

Lt. Forsythe said, "We will stop here men. Find good cover on each side of the trail, and we will stay hidden tonight and wait for news from our scouts. No fires and no noise."

I awoke to the voice of the Lieutenant. He waved his hands in an agitated conversation with one of the scouts. I couldn't make out exactly what he said, but he wasn't being quiet, and he didn't sound happy.

The Oneida shrugged his shoulders and melted away into the woods. Our lieutenant yelled out, "pick up your bedroll and get your gear together. We are heading for home."

"What about the raiders, Lieutenant?"

"They went back to Oswegatchie."

"Did they learn we were coming for them?"

"No. It turns out they were apparently only a large hunting party. But you men did an outstanding job, and if they had come we would have butchered them. I'm proud of you. Now let's go home, you've done your duty."

The anticlimactic journey back gave me plenty of time to think about Penelope. In the future, I would use the Campbell's carriage. I was reasonably sure George wouldn't mind, and I wanted a more comfortable means of transportation for Pen. He had given me permission to use any of the farm equipment I needed, and I convinced myself it was okay to lump the carriage into that agreement. I posted a letter to George letting him know about my plans. I didn't know when or if he might receive it, but it made me feel better.

I endured seven hard days away from Penelope, and I yearned to see her, but first I needed a good night's rest in my own bed. I slept like the dead, and I awoke stiff as a rail. Eager to get to the Archer's, I didn't bother with breakfast. Instead, I saddled my horse and set out.

Ananias came to the door and smiled. "Good to see you back. You are out early."

"I would like to speak to Penelope. Is she up yet?"

"She's not here. Her father picked her up and took her home. Have you had breakfast?"

"No I haven't. Will she be coming back?"

"Come on in and have a bite. We'll talk about it."

The smoky, pervasive air of frying bacon clinched the invitation, but more importantly, I needed to learn about Penelope. It pleased Elizabeth to see me. "Welcome, Jacob. It's good to see you back safely. I am sorry you missed Penelope. Her father came to get her day before yesterday. She wanted to stay, but he said mother needed her. She left a letter for you."

She handed me the letter, which I opened immediately, and started reading:

"Dearest Jacob, I prayed for your safety every day. I was so afraid something might happen to you. If you are reading this right now, my prayers have been answered. Mother is not well, and I must leave before you have gotten back. You have been very kind to me, and in the short time we have had together I have grown very fond of you. I hope to see you again. Yours Truly, Penelope."

I read it twice and tucked it into my jacket pocket.

"Sit down Jacob. Would you like a cup of coffee?"

"Yes. It smells wonderful, and so does that bacon. I wasn't hungry until I came in, but now I'm starved. So tell me about Penelope. Will she come back here this fall?"

"That depends on you. If you want her to come back, I'm sure she will. It seems you were all she talked about after you left. Well, you and your mother that is."

"How do I let her know I would like her to come back?"

"If I were you, I'd take a ride down to their farm and ask her personally, and you could meet my in-laws."

"I'll need directions. I only know the general area where she lives

Chapter 19

Meeting Mr. and Mrs. Jecocks

The ride to the Jecocks' consumed the better part of the morning; Silas sometimes trotted, sometimes walked. Indian summer bathed us in sunshine, making the journey all that much more enjoyable. My horse wasn't growing any younger, but with a few breaks, he didn't have any difficulty getting us there. I paid close attention to the roads because on my next trip I wanted to take the carriage if the way appeared acceptable. I reined Silas up in front of the farmhouse about midday, fastened him in the shade, and knocked at the door.

A gentleman, who I assumed was Penelope's father, answered. "Can I help you?"

"Yes, sir. I'm Jacob Morrissey; I came to see Penelope."

A smile spread across his face. "Well bless my soul, I've heard a lot about you, but I didn't know you were coming. I'm Harold Jecocks, Penny's father. Come in, come in. You've had a long ride; can I get you something to drink? Some cider perhaps?"

"Cider would be fine, Mr. Jecocks. I am a bit dry. Is your daughter home?"

"Certainly, I guess you came to see her, not to gab with me. I'll let her know you are here."

He left me sitting alone, and while I waited, a large hound walked into the room and eyed me. I took a piece of jerky from my pocket and held out my hand. "Here boy. I've got something for you."

Wagging his tail, he walked to my hand and cautiously took the offering. It must have hit the spot, because he smelled my leg and then rubbed up against me. I patted his head and scratched behind his ear.

"I see you have met Bay." It was Penelope with a cup of cider.

"I thought father was kidding with me when he said you were here. What a wonderful surprise. I had been hoping you might come, but I didn't really expect it. Will you spend the night?"

"If it is acceptable to your folks, I would appreciate doing that. I'm sure Silas will as well. It's been a long day for him." I sipped the cider. It was tingly, just starting to harden, but still sweet. Just the way I like it best.

Harold came back into the room with his wife. "Jacob, this is Penny's mother, Amelia."

"I'm pleased to meet you, Mrs. Jecocks. I hope you don't mind my dropping in, but Ananias said I should."

"Not at all. I can see why my daughter is so taken with you. Did you come all this way to see my daughter, or do you have business down this way?"

"My only purpose was to see her. She left before we had returned from our scout; I didn't get to wish her goodbye."

"Will you spend the night with us?"

"I will if you don't mind putting me up."

"You could stay longer, if you wish." Said Harold

"That's very kind of you, sir, but there are many things to take care of before winter arrives. I would not be much of a farmer if I let them slide."

"I understand completely. I am still harvesting myself. By the way, do not be surprised if Bay crawls into bed with you tonight. If you wake up and he's there, just push him off and tell him to git."

I finished my cider, and told Penelope I needed to take care of Silas and get him settled for the night. She came with me, and we led my worthy steed to the barn for water, hay, and a cup of oats. I closed the gate on his stall and Pen quit waiting for me, throwing herself into my arms.

My pent up desire exploded. Pulling her tight against me, I kissed her for the very first time, and the second and third. I nuzzled her neck with my lips, caressing her cheek with my afternoon stubble and running my right hand through her hair, slightly massaging her scalp. My hand dropped lower to her shoulder blades and the small of her back, and stopped on her buttocks.

I must have overplayed my hand. Pulling away, she said, "We had better go back to the house or my parents will suspect we are doing more than bedding down your horse."

The night was clear, and for a while we stood outside holding hands and marveled at the brightness of the stars and the Milky Way. Orion, Cassiopeia, and the Northern Cross stood out brilliantly, but the temperature hovered just above freezing. We called it quits and surrendered to the lure of the home's warmth. That night, the house wasn't terribly cold, but neither was it all that warm, and I was glad for the blankets and heavy quilt on my bed. Warm and exhausted, I went to sleep rather quickly, but sometime after midnight I woke to Bay burrowing his way into my covers. "Git out of here."

"Are you sure you want me to?"

Chapter 20

That's not Bay

"Move over Jacob. I need a little room."

The bed became warmer. I turned on my side to face her, and she snuggled up against me. The purposeful, soft pressure of her breasts against my chest summoned the memory of my afternoon in the hayloft. I thirsted for her; my body reacted to her presence, but she began to speak.

"Jacob, I didn't come here for that; although, I did want to feel what it would be like to share your bed, but I want to talk. You must know I love you. I have since we went to church. You are all I could ever want in a man. Am I wrong about you? Do you wish to have me as a wife, or am I just another woman passing through your life? I have to know."

"No, I would like for us to pass through this life together. Last summer I didn't believe I would ever feel this way again, but I do love you. Will you marry me?"

"Yes, you know I will, but first you must ask my father." Slipping out from under the bedding, she suggested, "Do it in the morning." And she disappeared from my room.

My disappointed body calmed, but sleep returned. I awoke to the irresistible smell of breakfast and dressed quickly. It turned out to be more of a feast than a breakfast, and after my second cup of coffee, in the presence of Penelope and her mother, I completed my task.

"Mr. Jecocks, I'm in love with your daughter. I would like your permission to marry her. I promise I would be a good and faithful husband to her."

"Jacob, if you will spend today with me, and spend one more night with us, I will give you my answer tomorrow. If you will bear with me, I would like to get to know you better."

It was not the answer I had been expecting. "Very well, I can understand your concern, and I would like the chance to get to know you too. I would be honored to spend another night in your home."

"Thank you, Jacob. You won't be sorry I'm sure."

We saddled our horses and took a leisurely ride around his property. It was well kept and already partly plowed for spring. We talked as we rode. "Tell me, Jacob, can you afford a wife?"

"Yes, sir. I own my own farm, and I manage an additional parcel as well. We are not rich, but we do not lack either. Penelope will have everything she wants or needs."

"You know she has a bad arm?"

"Yes, I knew that from the day I met her. It is more of a concern for her than it is for me, but it is nothing to be ashamed of. It makes no difference to me."

"I am pleased to hear that. I have often told her the same thing. When she marries, she will have a small dowry, and she has a hope chest and a blanket box. She made the quilt you slept under last night. She is an excellent seamstress"

"I know. She made the dress she wore the night I met her. It was beautiful. My mother says she does the finest work she has ever seen."

"Your mother lives with you? How does Penny feel about that?"

"They hit it off wonderfully. They are like two peas in a pod. I don't know which one she cares most about, mother or me."

We rode on quietly into a shallow valley. I could see the silvery sheen of a stream at the bottom. "Do you do any fishing, Jacob?"

"I have, but not a lot."

"Well the stream ahead is overflowing with brook trout. What would you think about catching a few for dinner after lunch?"

"Sounds like fun to me."

Out of nowhere he asked, "Jacob, did my daughter come into your bedroom last night?"

For a moment I thought about lying, but I answered truthfully. "Yes."

"Did she sleep with you?"

"No, sir. She came in to talk. I asked her to marry me, and she told me to ask you today, and then she left." I conveniently left out the rest."

"You will have your chance to spend the night with her; we have decided you and Penelope should bundle tonight. You will have plenty of opportunity to talk."

I knew about bundling, but I hadn't expected it. I didn't want to tell him we had sort of done that already, at least for a short time.

The trout fishing was nowhere as exciting as the thoughts of sleeping with my intended that evening. We did catch trout, and we kept eight of them that were each about 12 inches long. "This will be enough for dinner." He said as he cleaned the beautifully colored fish.

Dinner featured the trout, fried golden brown, accompanied by boiled potatoes and glazed carrots. A mouthwatering bread pudding with maple syrup completed the meal.

Mrs. Jecocks said, "Penelope prepared the bread pudding and the trout."

"I've never had better. She is a fine cook."

We sat visiting in the parlor following dinner. Mr. Jecocks said, "Pen tells me you are a militia man. Do you believe you fellows can stand up to the British if it comes to that?"

"I'm sure we can. I was away on a scout looking for Indians who had been reported when you came for your daughter, and our lieutenant told us we had done a great job."

"Did the Indians give you much of a fight?"

"No. They turned around and went back north before we could even catch up with them."

"Is your father in the militia?"

"My father died more than three years ago, but he had been a captain in the militia and fought in the war against the French. He was badly wounded, but he survived. That was why Sir William deeded him our land outright."

"So it's been just you and your mother since then?"

"Yes, sir. I run the farm and work our oxen pulling stumps. We have made out well."

The time dragged by. I don't know what thoughts ran through Penelope, but mine gravitated around what would happen later that night, and it seemed like we were wasting time. Her mother left us for a moment returning with a blanket of some kind. "Harold, I think it's time to allow Penny and her guest to go to bed. I've got the bundling bag right here; let's get them upstairs."

The bag was actually two blankets sewn together and then sewn down the center creating two attached bags which was spread on the bed. There was a draw string at the top of both sections. Pen, in her night gown, got into one side, and I crawled into the other, wearing my long johns.

Her parents drew the top together and covered us with a thick quilt, wished us goodnight, and just like that we were alone together. I kissed her and then we talked. "Father and mother bundled before they were married. I think it is a tradition."

"It's sort of a confining tradition."

"That's the idea, but the game is, how does one overcome the restraints?"

I jumped, feeling her hand touch me. I reached down and grabbed it. "How did you do that?"

"Simple, a good seamstress is never without her shears. I just cut the string."

"So now what do we do?"

"Use our imagination."

Chapter 21

The Answer is Yes

A knock at the door woke us. "May I come in?" asked her father.

"We wish you would and get us out of this contraption." Pen replied.

Entering the room, his eyebrows rose. He untied us, more than a little surprised I believe, that we had not wiggled loose somehow. "How did you sleep?"

"Oh, very well." She said. "We talked until we were worn out and then drifted off. We are starving though."

We had an interesting breakfast. They didn't want to ask about our night, but curiosity was written all over their faces. They danced around the edges asking things like, "Did you get to know each other better?"

Pen took pleasure in answering for us without giving out any real information. "Much better."

"Do you think you will live happily together?"

"Together?" She smiled, "I believe we will."

"Amelia must have done a very good job of making your blanket. Were you comfortable?"

"Extremely."

I broke into the conversation. "Mr. Jecocks, you said you would give me your answer this morning. Will you give us your blessing to get married?"

"I do—wholeheartedly. When would you like to marry?"

Pen provided a solid answer, "A week from Saturday."

"And where would you like to have the ceremony?"

"Right here in our home."

"Is that acceptable to you, Jacob?" He asked.

"Perfectly, sir. I will come back the day before and bring my mother. I know she would not want to miss it."

"Then it's settled. We will look for you a week from this Friday."

Penelope beamed as her mother hugged her, and then hugged me as well, and whispered in my ear before turning me loose. "My wish for you is found in Genesis 1:28, and I look forward to the day."

Finishing breakfast, I went to see to my horse. He was reluctant to leave his stall, but Pen had come out bringing a carrot for Silas that brought him forth, and I saddled him. I held her hand as we led him back to the house. Her mother came out with a bag and handed it to me. "This is for your trip. It should keep your belly from gnawing your backbone."

"Thank you. I will enjoy it I am sure."

"There are a few carrots for your horse too."

I fastened the bag to my saddle, gave Penelope a kiss, and mounted my steed. "I will see you a week from Friday."

I drew back on the reins at the top of the hill and looked back. I could see her still standing outside the house waving. I took off my hat, waved it over my head, and resumed my journey. To help pass the time, I thought about all the events that had led up to this point, all of the what-ifs. There were so many things that could have taken place that would have made our meeting, much less our wedding, highly unlikely. If my father had not been severely wounded in the French and Indian War, he would have remained a captain of the militia, and William Campbell would never have come to take that position, and I never would have met Ellie. If he had come, but hadn't been a Loyalist, I would have married Ellie. If she had not to Canada with him, we would have married.

If I had gone to Connecticut with George, I wouldn't have joined the Tryon County Militia, and I wouldn't have met Ananias Archer or Elizabeth, and then I never would have met Penelope. There were many other things that could have made a difference as well, but my head started rebelling against the task, and I gave up.

Some people claim everything happens for a reason or a purpose, others say it is just by accident or chance. I don't know which is right, but whatever it was that brought us together, I was grateful.

Even before we got to Johnstown, Silas knew where he was and where he was headed. He picked up the pace. Smoke curled from the chimney, and mother was coming out of the barn. The sounds of the horse turned her to see us.

"Hello, Mother. We are back."

"Yes, I can see that. I thought you would be back yesterday."

"It got late, and the Jecocks' asked me to stay the night. All in all, it was a very enjoyable trip. Pen and I are going to be married a week from Saturday. I will take you down in the carriage the day before."

"That's pretty sudden, but it doesn't surprise me at all. I knew the two of you were made for each other when I met her. Where will you live?"

"Why here, of course. This is my home, our home."

"Good. It gladdens my heart to hear that. You may have to put an addition on the cabin, but that's a small thing. Now come inside and have something to eat."

"I'm not too hungry mother, the Jecocks made a huge lunch for me to eat along the way."

"So put the horse away and come inside. You can at least have a cup of coffee and tell me all about your experience."

Once I told her almost everything I could remember, she said, "Tell me what impressed you the most about Penelope."

"There were two things besides her beauty, her wit, and her ability to use her shears."

Chapter 22

The light weight of the carriage compared to our wagon allowed Silas to trot easily, even with mother along. We had all day, so we took several rest stops. I believed Pen would be pleased. She knew we were coming, of course, but I'm sure she expected the old buckboard. My stylish conveyance would be a surprise. With each mile we put behind us, my desire to hold her in my arms increased.

The late October night had painted the vegetation and fence rails along the road with hoar frost, which sparkled in the sun until being vaporized by its warm caress. Silas ignored the morning's cold fingers, while we shivered until the sun was well up, but I would not be cold that night.

The afternoon sun cast long shadows where we paused to look at the tidy, welcoming farm in the flats. I recognized it immediately, though I had only seen it one time before. I resisted the urge to hurry my horse along, and we maintained our steady pace until we pulled up under the chestnut tree beside the house. I was anxious to get Silas into a stall with some water and fresh hay. It had been a long day for all of us.

"Jacob!" Pen ran across the yard and wrapped her arms around me. "I thought you were never going to get here. Are you tired? We have some dinner for both of you on the table."

"That sounds great. Would you take mother inside, tell her to go ahead and eat. I want to get Silas out of the traces and get him taken care of first. He worked a lot harder today than I did."

"I'll come out as soon as your mother is settled. Your horse can stay in the same stall he did before. I already have hay and water out for him."

Silas munched his hay, and shivered with pleasure, while I wiped and brushed him. Pen came in with a carrot for Silas. "It will take me a few more minutes to wipe him down and get him comfortable. Then we can go inside."

"That's one of the things that makes me love you so. You are kind, patient, and considerate with me and my family, with just about everyone really, even your horse and your oxen. Now tell me, did you buy the carriage just for me? I will feel like a real lady riding in it."

"I would like to say yes, but it is from the Campbell farm, and I will have use of it until George Campbell comes home. Lord only knows how long that will be. Probably not before the war ends."

"Maybe by then we will be able to afford our own carriage." She hinted.

Most of the time from dinner until our wedding the next morning was sort of a blur. No matter what was said or what our parents did, it escaped me. We sat together holding hands, content, but excited and filled with one another. Thoughts of her preoccupied my mind. I wondered if Pen might slip stealthily into my room during the night. She didn't, but Bay did, and he snored. I swore it would be the last night I would sleep with a dog.

The preacher arrived in time for a free breakfast; a likeable gentleman, and we talked a while about marriage and the responsibilities of a good husband. He had known Penelope since her birth, and was close to the family and Elizabeth and Penelope. The ceremony, if one could call it that, was quite short. Only families with lots of money and influence had elaborate affairs with many guests and a celebratory meal afterwards.

The pastor departed after lunch, and we all settled down to take a breather. We had decided the three of us would leave the next morning, so we could be home before dark without putting too much pressure on poor old Silas. We wouldn't load the carriage too heavy because the Jecocks' said they would bring Pen's hope chest, blanket box, and a few other items up the following weekend and spend a few days with Elizabeth and their granddaughter, Amy.

The sun had barely dipped below the horizon, and lanterns were lit, but Pen and I had no intention of spending the evening visiting. "Mr. Jecocks, my wife and I are rather tired and would like to retire. We want to be fresh in the morning so we can get an early start right after breakfast. If you will please excuse us, we are going upstairs now. We will see you in the morning."

Pen giggled when I closed the bedroom door behind us. "You had better not be too tired, Mr. Morrissey, or I will be extremely disappointed."

"Don't you worry, Mrs. Morrissey, I'll never be too tired for you. Now, do you want me to snuff the candle before you get undressed and into your night clothes?"

She said nothing for a moment. "Yes, Jacob. Let's keep a little mystery between us about ourselves just for this night."

"As you desire, my love." The room was dark. I removed my clothes, including my long johns, and pulled my nightshirt down over my head. I was the first beneath the quilt. My heart pounded. I felt the cover lift, the bed moved under me, and she was in my arms.

I felt her hands pull up my nightshirt and slide across my chest and down my back, moving slowly, lingering here and there, and exploring my body, driving me nearly crazy with desire. I could hear her breath quivering as she inhaled and exhaled. I sought her lips and found them seeking my own. She took my hand in hers and placed it on her breast. Firm and hot, her nipples stood out like acorns. I could hear and feel the thumping of my heart in my head. She was not wearing a night gown.

She rolled over and we became one as man and wife. It was exquisite, but it ended all too quickly. We lay side by side gasping and shivering with emotion and pleasure.

Our fingers traced lazy circles and lines on each other's body. It was gentle, sweet, and enticing. She giggled as I swung my leg over hers. "Again, so soon? You lied, you weren't tired at all."

We came together once more, slowly, gently at first, then with passion and she arched up against me, urging me on until she dug her fingernails into my back, pressing me against her as her body convulsed. "Wow," she gasped. "That was incredible."

Chapter 23

The New Mrs. Morrissey

The loft served as our bedroom for about two weeks. Ananias recruited a few militia men to help add a room to our cabin. I requisitioned some of the lumber stacked in the barn at Blessed Hope, plus enough cedar shingles to cover the roof, and a window that was left over when the barn had been built. First, our team put up three log walls enclosed against the west side of the house. One wall had an opening for a window. We built the rafters, framed in the roof and added the courses of shingles. Ananias and I finished it from there.

He helped cut a doorway out of the cabin wall providing access to the room, and we completed the room by setting the window, smoothing the dirt, putting in floor joists, and laying down a pine plank floor. It was rough, but it would mean we no longer had to climb a ladder to get to our bed.

"It's wonderful, Jacob. I'll sew a curtain for the window, and we can move our bed. Is it finished now?"

"Not exactly. I still have to caulk the walls. We don't want cold wind and snow hitting us while we sleep this winter. I'm just going to do the inside for now, but I will finish the job on the outside in the spring. I'm only sorry I don't have something better for you."

"Don't be. This is our first very own room, and as long as you are sleeping by my side, I will never complain. I have never been happier than I am right now."

"May I see your room too?" Mother had come up from behind.

"Of course you can. It still needs some work, but it will be just fine for us."

"The cabin didn't look much different than this when your father built it, but we turned it into a home. You will too."

Ananias helped me move the bed into our room, and he gave us a small stand he had built as a wedding present. Penelope's parents brought her hope chest, blankets, and the rest of her clothes. They stayed for several days with Ananias and Elizabeth, admiring and complimenting their granddaughter. Little Amy cuddled with them and babbled; they hugged and kissed her and sang to her. Her vocabulary was still limited, but she already called them Papa and Nama. Pen and I speculated what lay ahead, foreseeing the days when we would have little ones of our own to share with both of their nanas, and their papa.

The morning the Jecocks's left, the sky threatened to open up, and they shivered; the sharp, North Wind pierced their clothing. Pen gave them one of our blankets to wrap up in on their way home. There were tears in her eyes. We knew we would be unlikely to see them again until weather broke in the spring. The war continued, and unbelievably, so far we remained unmolested. What little we heard indicated things were not going well for General Washington and his men. I couldn't help but wonder how George was doing and if he was well.

The howling of the wind increased that night, rattling the window in our room, searching for even the smallest entrance, but the caulking did its job. We enjoyed each other once more under the quilts, and fell asleep gratified and happy.

Toward morning, the wind blew itself out, and I awoke and got out of bed without disturbing Pen. I put some kindling on the coals in the fireplace, and once it blazed up, I added several larger pieces of wood. It took a while to take the chill off the cabin.

"Mmm, that feels good." Mother stood beside me, hands stretched out toward the fireplace. "How about my making some breakfast? I'll be happy to stay near the fire while you get your wife up."

"I'm up. I'll help you, Mother." She stood in the doorway to our room. If there was ever a vision of pure loveliness, she exceeded it. I could not conceive of a life without her; of all men, I was the most fortunate.

****

One morning on my way to the barn, I saw a movement in the brushy swale down the hill. I casually retraced my steps to the cabin. Pen said, "That was quick. Is there a problem?"

"I'm not sure. I saw something moving in the brush behind the barn. It might be an Indian or maybe just my imagination, but I'm taking my rifle to the barn."

I loaded the rifle and stepped back outside. I slipped to the left in order to put the barn between me and the brush. It might be one Indian, possibly more. My mouth tasted like cotton, my chest tightened, and I realized I trembled slightly as I reached the barn. Going inside, I climbed the ladder into the loft and moved to the mow door and opened it just a crack. I had a perfect view of the swale.

I poked the gun barrel out through the crack and steadied my rifle against the frame, settling my sights on the brown form in the swale. I took a breath, let half of it out and squeezed the trigger.

I ran out of the barn and back to the cabin. I opened the door and found myself staring at the muzzle of a musket. Mother lowered the gun. "Whew! I thought you were an Indian coming through the door."

"I'm glad you took time to make sure. Now I need my knife. Would you get it for me while I reload my rifle?"

"Did you get him?" She asked.

"Yes, but I wanted to reload the rifle in case I only wounded him."

"Why do you need the knife?

"I need to gut him."

Her jaw dropped. "Why in God's name would you gut an Indian?"

"No mother, I didn't shoot an Indian. I shot a deer, a nice big buck. He was browsing on the brush. I'll dress him out and pull him up to the barn. We will have fresh liver tonight."

Chapter 24

I skinned and quartered the fat buck and hung the meat in the smokehouse. I carried the tongue, neck, liver, and heart into the cabin, and mother and Penelope took over.

Mother took control. "Jacob, slice some bacon and bring it in; Penelope get a couple onions and three or four potatoes."

I returned to the smokehouse, took down a slab of bacon and cut loose six thick slices before hanging it back up. The salty, smoked bacon, hams, and sausage were staples during winter months. The new venison would be a welcome change. I planned to jerk some of it, but the rest would keep just fine hanging until we used it.

"Here's your bacon. It's getting miserable outside. I've never seen it so cold this early in December. It's probably going to be one hard winter. I'm glad I put in a good supply of firewood. How about some sauerkraut with dinner?"

Delicious tendrils of onion and bacon swirled around the cabin, riding on the earthy smell of frying liver. Pen brought a bowl of pickled cabbage from the sauerkraut barrel, and mother made gravy for the potatoes. No king ever ate any better.

Having my wife sharing my bed made December nights bearable while temperatures outside our cabin hovered around zero. I braved the elements twice a day caring for our livestock. It wasn't so bad once I got to the barn, but the short trip out and back to the necessary house was brutal for all of us, especially if the wind blew.

We led a life more like ground hogs hibernating in their tunnels, but we got a welcome thaw on January 10th.

Penelope suggested, "Jacob, let's go visit Ananias and Elizabeth before we get cabin fever."

"We could do that. I don't think he got a deer last fall, so I'll take him a front quarter of venison. We should take mother along too. I'll see if she would like to go."

She was ready for a change of scenery. "I'll pack up some of the scones Pen baked yesterday. I'll be ready to go as soon as you are."

Silas needed some exercise, but he was reluctant to leave his stall. I put my rifle in the sleigh, hooked him up, and in return he gave me a sad look, like "really?" Once we were on our way he perked up, and by the way he stepped out, I was pretty sure he enjoyed the exercise.

We surprised everyone seeing us out and about.

"Jacob, come in. We were just talking about you. Look who's here Amy. It's Uncle Jacob and Aunt Penelope."

She ran over and gave us hugs. I gave her a piece of maple sugar, and told Ananias, "Come to the sleigh with me, I've got something for you too."

He slipped on his coat. "I've got some news I heard in town yesterday. I'll share it with all of you when we are back inside. Now what do you have?"

I lifted the front quarter of venison from the sleigh and handed it to him. "I brought you some fresh venison and some jerky."

"Thank you. I know Elizabeth will be especially glad to have it, not that I won't. Let's hang it in the shed and we'll get back inside."

We shucked our coats in the cabin, and he shared his news. "General Washington fought a great battle at Trenton the day after Christmas. His army killed or captured more than a thousand Hessians, killed their commander in the battle, and captured 6 cannon. Your friend, George, was there. He's an aide to General Washington now, and he's the one who sent the news."

"Finally some good news. I was afraid when the army had to retreat south from New York, he was a goner. They must have captured supplies, shot and powder at

Trenton. Maybe he can keep going a while longer. Hold out for spring."

"I don't know about that, Jacob, but I am fearful about this coming summer. The Oneidas are already warning us we will be attacked by Mohawks and Onondagas, and very likely by the Seneca and Cayuga warriors as well."

"We'll be ready for them. I think our strength is about a thousand men, more than enough to deal with whatever they throw at us."

"But Jacob, they can hit us in so many places. We can't protect everyone or even every town."

"We will just have to let the officers figure that out. For now, the war seems to be far away, and a few Indian raids can be dealt with. Let's just count our blessings."

"You are a true optimist, Jacob. I wish I could be as confident as you are, but there will be fighting this year. I can feel it in my bones."

We shared dinner before we left for home. The ride was quiet, each of us lost in our own thoughts. I thought of Ananias's words about the Indians. He was likely right of course. The Indians would certainly test us, and we had no comprehensive plans for defense other than to call out the militia and react to any attack. We would be at a disadvantage, because there were so many areas where they could strike. I hoped we would have enough warning to be able to meet them head on.

I kept both my rifle and my father's army musket loaded in the cabin at all times, and I never went out without one or the other. My brother-in-law's words had made me paranoid, or at least extra cautious.

Two days later, a knock came upon our door. I opened it to discover George standing before me in a Continental Captains uniform. "George, you're home!" What a dumb thing to say; of course he was home, he stood right in front of me. "Why are you here? I thought you were in New Jersey or Pennsylvania."

"I was wounded at Princeton. The General sent me home to recover. The troops are in Winter Quarters now, and I could be spared. May I come in?"

"Yes, I'm Sorry, come in, come in."

Pen had never met him. "Penelope, this is George Campbell, a dear friend. George, this is my wife Penelope. You're a Captain now?"

"Pleased to meet you, I'm sure. And yes, I am a Captain."

He turned to Mother. "Pleased to see you, Mrs. Morrissey."

"It's good to see you again also. Did I hear you say you were wounded?"

"Yes, I received a bullet in the thigh, but it was a clean wound and our surgeon said it would be healed in about two weeks. He didn't like the idea of my riding, but he told me to keep the bandage tight on the wound and clean it when I got home."

"Does it hurt much?" she asked.

"No, it hurt like the O'Harry at first, but it's feeling better now. I stayed last night at Blessed Hope, but this afternoon I realized I was not going to be able to do everything on my own. I was wondering if I could lay out my bedroll on the floor in front of the fire, and stay here with you. I'd be glad to pay."

"Nonsense." Mother said. "You can stay here, but keep your money. We don't charge good friends."

"That's right." I told him, "and we would like to hear about what's been happening with you and the army."

Chapter 25

"I haven't had a decent meal for several weeks, and certainly none that smelled as good as that venison stew you're cooking, Mrs. Morrissey. It brings back memories of meals I shared with your family in better times.

"Well thank you, George, but I suspect your mother made just as good back then."

"Oh, she did. I miss our family meals and the fun we had together. It seems almost impossible that here I am serving in the Continental Army, while my family is in Canada, and my father is an officer in the Royal Yorkers. I believe he made a mistake, but the one thing I am particularly thankful for is he and I are unlikely to ever face each other on the battlefield. I don't expect the Yorkers will show up in New Jersey."

I had to ask him, "What's it like George? Being in a battle that is? Were you scared?"

"I think I was scared every time we were going into a fight. My mouth would get dry and I'd breathe faster, but when the shooting started, all I could think about was my men and my responsibilities. Things get very confused very quickly, and anyone who loses his head can be in real trouble. We just do what we have to do, what we are ordered to do. General Washington has gotten us out of some tight spots, and I'd follow him into Hades if he asked."

"I have this nagging thought that I may be too scared to fight when the time comes, that I might run. Do your men ever run?"

"Some do, sometimes we all do, but mostly we face up to the British, and they are the ones doing the running. Remember this Jacob; one can be shot in the back as easily as in the breast. There is a time for fighting, a time for standing your ground, but there is also a time when surrender or run are the only good options. It's better to live to fight another day, than to die for no good reason. I have run more than once, but not before further resistance was hopeless."

"So tell us about Trenton."

"General Howe and his army forced us out of New York even though we made them pay dearly, and we retreated into Pennsylvania. Times were tough for us, but the General received information that indicated we could surprise the Hessians in Trenton right after Christmas. We crossed the Delaware River during Christmas night and reached Trenton about first light on the 26th."

"How many Germans were there?"

"I think about 1400, but we surprised them with their pants down and their night clothes on. We had them cornered, and the fight was hot for a while once they got out of their barracks, but when their commander was killed, it pretty much took the starch out of them."

"How many men did we lose?"

"Believe it or not, none, not a one. We had four men wounded, but we killed and wounded around 115, and we captured 920 of the Hessians. We also took 6 cannons, and 19 stands of regimental colors. You know how they hate to lose them."

"And that was it?"

"No, not entirely. We captured a bunch of supplies and a lot of shot and powder. I'll tell you, that German sausage is good stuff and so is their beer. We took everything, including the prisoners, back across the river. We figured the British would come up from Princeton to retake the town, and they tried. You wouldn't believe it, but we went back across the river again before they got there and gave them a bloody nose when they tried to cross the little stone bridge over Assumpink Creek to close with us."

"So then you withdrew?"

"No. The British probably figured they could finish us off the next morning, so late in the day they ended the attack, but during the night we made a forced march around them and attacked the smaller force that had been left in Princeton. We killed about 80, wounded about 95 more and took about 200 of them prisoner. The rest escaped, and then we skedaddled back over the river. They didn't offer to follow us, but licked their wounds instead. We had faced British regulars, and we beat them. It was a real tonic for the men."

"So where were you wounded?"

"Right here," he said, "pointing to his right thigh."

"No, you fool; I meant what part of the fighting caused your injury?"

"The shooting."

"Come on. George. You know what I mean."

"It was in Princeton. Those redcoats put up a good fight even though we outnumbered them in men and cannons. But finally they broke and ran. Can you believe it? They were some of Cornwallis's soldiers, seasoned troops, the best they have, but they turned tail, and by then, we were exhausted and let them go."

"Where is the army now?"

"In Morristown. The British know where we are, but they don't campaign during the winter, so they are no threat to us until spring. We skirmish with foragers a bit, but usually no one gets hurt. I'll go back there to rejoin them as soon as my leg has healed enough."

The table was set, and the savory stew and fresh bread drew everyone's attention. George asked, "May I thank the Lord for his blessing?"

Jacob nodded.

"Lord, I thank you for good friends, for this wonderful meal, and for the loving hands which have prepared it. Please bless this food and be pleased with the conversation around this table. And Lord, give our men victory. In Jesus name. Amen."

Eating took priority over talking for a while, but George had some questions of his own. "Tell me, Jacob, how did you find such a beautiful bride, and how did you ever persuade her to marry a bumpkin like you?"

"She is the sister of Elizabeth Archer. Elizabeth is married to Ananias Archer, my best friend in the Militia. He and I farm your land together. He only lives a little way north of here. I don't know how I impressed her enough that she agreed to become my wife, but I thank the Good Lord every day for her."

"I always thought I would be your brother-in-law, and I would take you to Connecticut and make a lawyer out of you. Strange how things turn out isn't it? Here you are married to Penelope, my family is in Canada, I've been wounded fighting for liberty from the King they serve, and I'm sleeping on the floor of the man who worked for my father."

"Jacob, I would like you to ride over to Blessed Hope with me tomorrow morning. There are some things I need to share with you."

Chapter 26

George's Will

We walked our horses; there was no hurry in getting to Blessed Hope. It gave us time to talk along the way. "The loyalists are mostly gone, but I don't blame them for leaving. They were used rather badly by the committee of safety, and even if they tried to get along with the rest of us, all they met was suspicion and accusations. There are a few who have refused to knuckle under and stayed on, but anyone who befriends them is roundly criticized. I can't help but feel it is wrong."

"Beware Jacob, even such innocent talk in the presence of some people might smack of treason. The time for talk and friendship with Loyalists has passed, and there is little chance of reconciliation until this war ends, if ever."

"I guess it is human nature, or perhaps our worst nature, to attack people who disagree with us, but I really believe that some who have been driven out would have joined our cause if treated differently."

"Again beware. Your loose tongue and thoughts will not help the loyalists, but they could destroy you."

"Do you think any of them will return after the war?"

"Do you mean like my parents and Ellie?"

I nodded, "Yes and others."

"If we win, and I think we will, I expect the big land owners will not be allowed to return. Men like the Johnson's will never get their land back. My father, I doubt he would want to. Those with a cabin and a little land may be allowed back, but I wouldn't count on it."

"So that was why your father sold his land and home to you?"

"Yes. He wasn't taking any chances. I would have inherited the land in any case, and by buying it, no one could take it away. It doesn't hurt now that I am an officer in the army either; although, I suspect it would not sit well with Father."

"He really wanted me to go with them, you know. Ellie did too. I tried to persuade her to stay, but she refused."

"You couldn't know it, but she begged father to let her stay. It didn't change her circumstances, but when they left, she nearly ran away to be with you."

I was silent.

What if she had come to me? What would life be like? What about Penelope?

Considering all the 'what ifs' left my mind spinning. None of that mattered in the end. Nothing would erase the past; one must live for the present and hope for the future.

We tied our horses to the hitching post and went inside. The house was cold and musty. There was wood, and George started a fire. We sat close to it while the house slowly warmed.

"Would you care for a brandy to warm you up inside?" He asked.

"I don't think there is any here. Either they took the spirits with them, or someone came in and pilfered them."

"You just didn't know where to look. Wait and I'll be back with glasses and a bottle."

He went into the library and returned a few minutes later holding a bottle of brandy. He poured us each a glass. "Here you are, my man. I'll show you where it's hidden before we leave."

We sat sipping the cold brandy. I seldom drank, and it burned all the way down.

He held up his glass toward the flames in the fireplace and said, "This is cognac, my father's favorite after dinner drink. It's good after coming in from the cold as well. It is usually served at room temperature."

"You got it just right then."

He gave me a strange look, and then laughed. "I meant it is usually served warm, not chilled. Now let's get to the things I need to share with you. First of all, even before I was wounded, I knew there was the possibility that I might be killed. I made out my will and left the original at my office in Hartford with my partner. I made three copies; one to keep here in the house, one for you to keep at home, and one in Albany. Each one has been signed and witnessed. If I die, I want you to be my executor, and you are also my main beneficiary. The house, land, equipment and home items will be yours. I have left a few things for Ellie if she returns."

"I don't know what to say, but I certainly hope you will take good care of yourself and avoid getting shot. I would prefer to have you as a friend for the rest of my life rather than your property."

"I know that, but just in case. Now there are two other things. The family silver is buried under the north end of the corn crib, and I have no objection to your using my carriage. How do you like the ride from those German made springs?"

"Your silver should be safe, but I'll keep an eye out for anyone poking about. I have enjoyed the carriage very much, and Penelope is thrilled with it. Can't say as I blame her, it rides like a boat on calm water."

"I'm pleased, and I'm also pleased at how you have kept the farm in good shape. Was it a good harvest this year?"

"Yes, Ananias and I realized a good crop. Thank you."

"That's quite alright. Now if you will come with me I'll put this Brandy away. You can see what we've got."

"I won't bother it while you are away."

"If you should want to, remember, I don't mind."

The return trip was filled with talk about mutual friends, our youthful hunting and fishing adventures, and the crazy things we had done. For the next 10 days we did a lot of reminiscing, spent part of a couple days visiting Ananias, and he had stopped limping. His wound healed quickly, and all too soon, he told us he would be leaving the next day.

He donned his uniform, saddled his horse, and packed his bedroll and saddle bags all before breakfast. Penelope cooked a big one, and at the same time, put together a hefty lunch for him.

"You know, I've put on weight this week. My uniform is a little tight, but a few days back with the men will take care of that. You have been patient and generous, and I am sure I have healed more quickly than I could have anywhere else."

I walked him out to his horse, and he said to me, "Jacob, I had a dream one night in the field, I saw my father, and he said to me, 'Neither one of us will survive this war. I miss you.' It was clear as a bell. That was when I knew I had to make plans in case it wasn't just indigestion. I love you and your mother, and Penelope is a peach. I love this North Country, and sometimes I get homesick. I hate to think this might be the last time I ever see it. Pray for me when you think of it."

He mounted his horse and rode off toward town. A chill swept over me, I had had the same dream about them.

Chapter 27

George Returns to the Continental Army

Our home settled back into a daily routine after his departure. I wanted to share the things that George had done and told me about, but I just couldn't tell them about the dream. I couldn't share the information about his premonition or his last will. It didn't seem right somehow.

Penelope asked me what we had done at his home. "You were gone for some time the other day. What did you do?"

"We got a fire started, had a glass of brandy, and looked around the house to make sure everything was in order. We talked about the days when we hunted and fished together, when things were pleasanter. He said you were a peach.

"He looked a little sad when he left. Is his leg completely healed?""

"Yes, his leg is fine. It's just that the world has changed so much, and will change even more in the days ahead. It lies heavy on his heart and mind. He longs for something that will never be again."

"Did he mind that we have been using his carriage?"

"No, not at all. He said he was pleased that we enjoy it. He seems to hold all things with a loose grip."

"Well I'm glad he stayed with us. He was a pleasure to have around, and he looks so masculine in his uniform. Why is it that he has not married?"

"I don't know. I've never asked him; I figure it's none of my business."

"You aren't thinking about running off and joining the army with him are you?"

"No, I could've done that before we met, but I believed my place was here, and I believe it even more now."

We didn't talk about him much after that, but we did pray for him nearly every night as January wore away into a bleak February. There was no news about Washington and his army, but that meant little. The British were known to be wroth to venture forth in the winter for battle, and the tired Continentals had no desire to provoke them.

Winter lost his grip on New York in early March, and Pen asked if we could journey to see her family. She had asked for little since we had been married, so I agreed, even though I would rather have waited until April.

"I'll take you and mother to see your family. I'll see if I can get Ananias to take care of the animals while we are gone."

"Mother spoke up. "No, I'll stay. I don't particularly like traveling at this time of year."

"Are you sure? I think they would enjoy seeing you again."

"I'll wait until summer, if you don't mind. I'll be fine here while you are gone."

The roads were muddy in places and snow covered in others, but Silas pulled the carriage through it all with a minimum of complaint.

"Is there any particular reason why we are going now instead of waiting a month or so?"

"I want to talk with mother. There are some things I really need her advice on, and I'm a little bit homesick. I expect they may be missing me too."

"I'm sure you are right, and I don't mind taking you. There is nothing I wouldn't do for you if it is within my power."

We traveled on, but then she cried out. "Oh Jacob, stop would you?"

"What's the matter? Don't you feel well?"

"I feel fine, but look at those pussy willows. Aren't they lovely? My mother always had a bouquet of them on the kitchen table. Would you stop and pick some for me?

"Here, hold the reins. I'll get you a bunch." I had a dozen or so stems of them in no time.

She held them in her lap and stroked the grey, fuzzy buds. "They are so soft, like a kitten or a baby's skin."

We continued on as she ran her fingers over the catkins. "Feel of them, Jacob. Aren't they soft?"

"Yep, they are, that's a fact."

"They are as soft as your baby's skin will be."

"What's that?"

"We are going to have a baby. That's what I want to talk with mother about."

"A baby? We are going to have a baby? Are you sure?"

She nodded her head and put her hand on my arm. "Are you happy?"

"Of course I'm happy, but you could have just talked to my mother about it."

"I already have."

"She knows? You told her before you told me?"

"Yes, I wanted to make sure I was right about it."

"Wait a minute. Should you be making this trip over these roads?"

"It's perfectly safe; it won't harm me or the baby."

"Oh, Penelope, I love you so much, and this is such a surprise, but it is a wonderful one. When is the baby due?"

"The first week in August I think."

The balance of the ride was anticlimactic, but when Pen announced the glad tidings to her parents, the joy and excitement began anew. We spent three pleasant days with them. She used most of her time talking with her mother the first day, and her father and I got to know one another better. A baby seemed to draw everyone closer together.

We were barely back home when she asked to go to see her sister. "I would like to tell her we are going to have a baby." That made sense to me, so we went the next morning. "Hello, Uncle Jacob," Amy said as we walked through the door. Elizabeth took one look at Pen and cried out, Penny, you're with child."

"Who told you?" she asked.

"No one. I could see it. You're glowing like a new mother to be. When?"

"I believe it will be the first week in August."

"It will be a busy month. We are expecting a brother or sister for Amy the last of August. I'm so glad we are not only sisters, but neighbors as well."

"Really? You too? They will be able to grow up together. That's wonderful."

"I shook hands with Ananias. "Congratulations. Looks like we will all have our hands full."

"Yes, it will be something all right, but I'm worried we might also have our hands full with the British. Our Indians say there are rumors of big plans afoot to invade us this summer. They don't have any hard evidence or real information on where or when the attacks will come, but I would bet we will be in the thick of it this summer."

Chapter 28

Starting a Family

I couldn't dwell on his words, but I couldn't forget them either. If an attack should come from Oswego, we would be right in its path. Probably the same was true if they came from the St. Lawrence by way of Fort Oswegatchie. If the blow should fall to the east of the mountains, down Lake Champlain, it would be out of our district and might not involve us at all.

There was nothing I could do about any of it. I would plant my crops in the spring and hope I would be around to harvest them in the fall. If war swooped in with talons spread wide, I was as ready as I would ever be.

April showered us with intermittent rain and sunshine. The maple syrup season ended, and I impatiently waited for the fields to become warmer and drier.

Penelope said, "For heaven's sake, Jacob, quit your pacing and grumbling about the rain. It will stop when it is good and ready. You won't change it. Come here, sit down with me."

I sat beside her, and she took my hand in hers, placing it on her stomach. "Wait a minute. Don't move your hand. There, did you feel that?"

"Yes. That's the baby?"

"He just started kicking last night. It's amazing. I've never felt anything like it before. He feels like a very healthy boy."

"What makes you think it's a boy? How can you tell?"

"I can't really, but you are going to need a boy to help you work the farm, so that's what I ordered."

"Have you picked out a name for him too?"

"No. If it's a boy, I'll let you pick the name; if it's a girl, we will decide on it. How is that?"

"Fair enough, but I'll come up with several boys names I like, and we can choose which one sounds best."

Now that we agreed on the important things, it was time Ananias and I planned our planting schedules. By sharing the work, not only on the Campbell farm, but also on our own fields, we could plant continuously as each section came ready, leaving the moister areas for later.

May 23rd, found all our seed sown, and some of the first fields planted already had sprouts up five inches. The warm, dry May gave the corn a great start. June arrived with the promise of a good harvest, and no sign of the feared invasion.

We spent our days cultivating one field after another, and by June 21st, our corn was mostly knee high and growing rapidly. Our wives were growing rapidly also, and spent a lot of time with my mother. Amy had been born three years before, so Elizabeth shared her experience, and she and Mother helped Pen through the days and months of her first pregnancy.

On June 28th, a rider from the Essex County Militia brought a communication for General Herkimer from General Gates. "Burgoyne with 20,000 regulars, some Loyalist units, plus several hundred Indians, are on their way down from Canada. I believe he means to attack Fort Ticonderoga, move south on Lake Champlain, and try to capture Albany. Be prepared to come to our need should I call for you."

I heard the news, pleased that the British were not coming here. At least our families were safe, I told Pen what was happening, but she didn't exactly understand.

"I don't want you to go."

"If we are ordered to go, we will have to, but they probably won't need us, we just have to be ready."

"When would you go?"

"I can't tell you, I have no idea when or even if we will go."

"Your son kicks every time he hears your voice. I want him to see you. I want you to hold him and sing to him. Isn't there any way you could stay here where it is safe?"

"If General Herkimer decides to leave a company or two behind to guard the people here, I might end up not going, but I don't know that."

The call for our services never came. The British captured Fort Ticonderoga on July 6th and made preparations to move south, but the militia and Continentals were making them earn their way. In Tryon County, we seemed to be living a charmed life. We cultivated our corn, tended our gardens and took care of our stock almost like it was peacetime.

From time to time, we heard about the campaign in the east. Burgoyne's juggernaut hesitated several times as it poured south. The British moved so slowly it allowed many more militiamen to join General Gates, swelling his numbers. Sooner or later they would clash. Maybe Tryon County would be spared.

The hopes and speculation in Tryon County were dealt a blow on July 17. The Continentals had taken some British prisoners, and learned from them there was another prong to Burgoyne's invasion. General Herkimer received the information and issued a warning that a possible British attack along the Mohawk River was a real possibility, and the Militia should be ready to turn out on short notice.

On July 30, Oneida Indians arrived, carrying disturbing news for General Herkimer; the anticipated British force was only four days away; he immediately issued a call to arms.

He questioned the Indians. "How many men do they have?"

"About 1800, British soldiers, Royal Yorkers, rangers and 800 Mohawk, Seneca, and other Indians."

"Did you learn anything about their plans?"

"They intend to seize and hold the Oneida Carry and lay siege to Fort Schuyler. After that, they will go down the Mohawk River and meet up with General Burgoyne and Lord Howe."

"Are you certain this information is accurate?"

"Yes. We have eyes and ears in his army."

"You have my gratitude. They will have to go through us first. That may not be as easy as they believe. They may not know there is a regiment of Continentals in the fort."

The militia gathered at Fort Dayton.

Ananias and I set out together for the muster. "I hate to go, Ananias. Penelope is going to have the baby any day now. I should be there."

"I know how you feel, but right now you are of more use to her by helping stop the British before they overrun us."

"Do you really think we can do it?"

"Continentals from the 3rd New York Regiment are garrisoned in the fort, and we will be outside to help them. I think between us we can hurt them enough that they will turn tail. We will see how many Militia men we have."

Chapter 29

Going to War

We walked into Fort Dayton mid-morning on August 3rd, joining about 500 others, with more arriving every few minutes. We located our company and regiment. The men claimed spots for the night and started to prepare their dinners. The tense atmosphere bespoke the trepidation infecting many of us, even as we foolishly boasted how we would give the British a drubbing, sending them back to Canada.

Colonel Fisher addressed us before sundown. "Men, all four regiments will be on the march tomorrow morning to relieve Fort Schuyler, approximately 40 miles from here. The General plans to attack the British force and trap them between us and the garrison. That means we will have to step lively, so get a good night's rest."

The heat of the night made a good night's rest elusive at best, impossible for some, and I felt like I had barely fallen asleep when the drummer beat reveille. Groans, coughs, and curses rent the air—threatening the drummer. Early dawn is an unpleasant time for many to wake, and the camp felt as though it would mutiny, but by seven-thirty, the first regiment was swinging out along the road. The rest of our ranks formed up, and we took our place in the column in order. The drums and fifes cheered us on our way.

Ananias and I marched side by side, on the left of our column. "You stay with me no matter what." He told me, but he didn't have to tell me, I had already determined I would stick to him like glue. The sun baked us, and our pace slowed considerably in the afternoon in spite of several rest stops. Late that afternoon, clouds blocked the sun, and brought a welcome breeze, but quite a number of our men had dropped out along the way earlier. Most of them would catch up in the evening. Some of our men were obviously out of shape. The British sun had done its best to stop us, but in spite of the heat, we made about 27 miles that day before stopping for the night.

It was a pleasure just to sit around the campfire and rub our sore feet after dinner. "That was one long trip today, Jacob. I thought we would stop earlier. The General and officers are riding horses, so it doesn't bother them to travel so far. They don't worry about us."

"I've been thinking about Penelope. I wonder if she had the baby yet."

"She's in good hands, you don't have to worry about her, and you'll be back home in a few days."

"Do you really think so? Just a few days?"

"Most battles don't last long. A day or maybe two, and win or lose it's done."

"Do you ever think you might be killed?"

"Jacob, stop worrying. No I don't think about it, and I don't worry about it. I will do the best I can to whip the British, and the best I can to stay alive. That's all we can do, and pray God will help us do both."

"I wasn't worried about being killed before Penelope and now the baby, but I would hate to leave them alone. If I do get killed, will you watch over them?"

"You aren't going to get killed. Stay with me and do what I tell you, and you will be fine. I don't intend to die, and you won't either. Now let's see if we can't catch up on our sleep."

I was jolted out of a sound sleep by reveille, but I felt a hundred times better than I had the morning before. It didn't hurt any either knowing we would have a shorter march that day. The late afternoon found us camping near Oriska, an Oneida Indian village. We still numbered nearly 800 militiamen, and all 15 of our supply and baggage wagons had arrived safely. We were about eight miles from

Fort Schuyler, so we expected to be fighting on the morrow.

Men from the First Regiment told us General Herkimer, earlier in the day, had picked three of their men for messengers, and sent them on ahead to sneak through the British lines, get to the fort, and alert Colonel Gansevoort, the Continental commander, that the militia was on its way, and would attack the next day.

Gansevoort was asked to fire three cannon shots on the 6th as a signal the messengers had arrived. When the cannon fired we would advance.

They didn't play that morning for fear it might catch the attention of the British, so our officers woke us. Conversations were in whispers even though it was hard enough just to hear each other, let alone alert the British.

"Do you have powder and balls enough for at least 8 shots?" Ananias asked me,

"Yes, I'm all set."

"I haven't noticed; do you have a tomahawk?"

"No."

"Get one before your next battle. Do you have a knife?"

"Yes."

"One more thing. Don't fire your gun unless you have a good shot. If you do, you are just wasting good powder and lead."

The sun came up and we still weren't moving out. Ananias said, "Seems to me it would be best to try to catch them early. I wonder what the holdup is."

"The officers are meeting right now; maybe I could get close enough to hear what they are saying."

No one paid any attention to me, and they argued loud enough that I could hear without being too close to call attention to myself.

The General insisted we should not move until after hearing the three cannon shots, but his officers disagreed with him.

"General, we should advance right now. If we wait we might be discovered and lose the element of surprise."

"No, I want to be sure the fort knows we are coming and will sally forth catching the enemy between us."

"I think that is unwise. When they hear the fighting, they will join us. There is no need to wait for a signal."

They ganged up on the General, and it sounded like he lost patience with his junior officers. Words became hotter and tempers flared.

"We can't act like cowards. Is there some other reason why you are so reticent?"

"Yes, General, does it have anything to do with one of your brothers serving with the enemy before us?"

"Some might say you have Tory or Loyalist sympathies."

The General exploded, "Get your men ready to march, but we are doing it against my better judgment. Colonel Cox, your First Regiment will be the Van, be sure they employ an advance guard. Colonel Klock, your Second Regiment will follow and support the First. Colonel Bellinger, your Fourth Regiment will be next with the wagons directly behind you. Colonel Visscher, your Third Regiment will compose the rear guard and protect the wagons. Assemble your units. You are dismissed."

Chapter 30

The Ambush

"We are going to be moving out very soon. We have been assigned to guard the rear and watch over the wagons. The General wanted to wait for the signal from the fort, but the officers said shameful things about him. He got hot under the collar and let them have their way."

"I don't really like it, Jacob. He knows what's best and decides the strategy; they should discuss it and accept his judgment. It's never good when the workers can tell the boss how a job should be done. It can become a bad habit. Mark my words; this will not turn out well."

We were about six miles from the fort at nine-thirty and General Herkimer halted the column and explained why. "We have a ravine ahead of us; it's the perfect spot for an ambush. We need scouts to confirm the area is free of the enemy. We must wait for that to be done before we proceed, or we will have to get off the trail and advance on both sides above it."

The reaction was immediate and humiliating to the General.

"The enemy doesn't know we are coming, why would they set up an ambush? Are you afraid of joining the battle at Ft. Schuyler?"

Another insubordinate officer offered, "Taking to the hillsides will slow us down at least two hours. We must push through."

"No one would try to ambush a column as strong as ours, it would be suicide."

The general tried reasoning with his officers. "We should at least send out flankers."

"By the time they get into position, we could be through the ravine. Are we men or cowards?"

Again, the infuriated General relented and the march continued against his better judgment. The men sprang to high spirits, egged on by their officers, and acted like in a victory march, instead of nearing a battle.

Ananias pulled on my sleeve, stepping out of the column, stooping down to take off a shoe.

Watching the regiment move by us, I asked, "Did you get a stone in your shoe?"

"No. Come with me."

We moved a short distance off the path, stepping behind a blueberry bush like we wanted to relieve ourselves. "Jacob, this is not right. The entire brigade is moving into the ravine, and we don't have any flankers out.

Follow me up the hill where we can see what's up ahead. I've got a bad feeling about all of this."

We got part way up the hill by the time our regiment had entered the ravine behind the slow moving wagons. Firing erupted, powder smoke from many guns drifted upward on both sides of the depression, and the screams of the Indians mingled with the anguished screams of wounded and dying men.

We ran ahead to see if we could help, but we were fired on by several Indians coming along the side of the hill our way. We were fortunate not to be hit. Ananias grabbed my sleeve again and pulled me down into a tiny depression. "Are you wounded?"

"No. What are we going to do?"

"We are going to find some cover behind that big chestnut with the stone beside it. It's not far. When I say run, you go and get behind the rock. If an Indian tries to shoot you, I'll take care of him." He took off his hat and pushed the muzzle of his musket up and cried, "run!"

I only took four or five steps before I heard his gun go off. A few more steps carried me to the cover, and I peeked over the rock. I saw Ananias jump up and run at me. At the same time an Indian stood up to draw a bead on him.

I reacted instinctively, getting off a shot at the warrior. He dropped backward, his gun going off as he fell, and Ananias landed beside me behind the stone. He started loading his weapon. "Jacob, don't just sit there, load your rifle; be quick about it now."

He reloaded and surveyed the forest. "Let me know as soon as you are done there. If I shoot, you take my place and keep any Indians from charging us. Then I'll do the same. You understand?"

"Yes, I understand, I'm ready now."

The shooting was heavier in the ravine, and smoke crept up the hill like fog. "I dropped the Indian who tried to shoot you. How did you do when I ran?"

"I hit one, but he was able to run away after."

"You've got a rifle, not like me and my musket. Take your time, and don't get so excited that you don't aim fine. We've got a couple working up on our left, and another was moving to get above us the last time I saw him. I can't see any more, but they could be out there just the same."

"Ananias, I can see one of the two you said were on the left. He's crawling, but I can't get a sure shot at him."

"Keep your rifle trained on him until he presents a shot. Yes, I can see him now. He's good at staying out of sight isn't he? As soon as I can get any kind of shot at him,

I'll give it a go. If I miss, he will probably try to rush us before I can reload. If he does he's close enough you should have a good shot."

I concentrated on the target, expecting Ananias to fire at any time. When his gun went off, the Indian only raised his head right into my sights, and I fired. Then I felt something strike heavily against my legs. I looked to my left and Ananias pounded the butt of his gun against the head of a bleeding warrior slumped in between us.

I was panting and shaking. "Did he jump in here when we shot?"

"No, I heard a noise behind us and turned. If he had a gun, one of us would be dead now, but he came charging with a tomahawk, and I blasted him just before he got to us. Did you get a shot?"

"Yes, I shot him in the head. He hasn't moved. What do we do now?"

He handed me the dead Indian's tomahawk. "Stick this in your belt. The day may come when you will be glad you have it. We could move down the hill and see if we could surprise some Indians from the rear."

"We don't have to look very far. The one I wounded is coming back with a bunch of his friends."

"Get that rifle loaded while you have the chance."

The savages spread out into a semi-circle, moving cautiously. Once they got behind us we wouldn't have much of a chance. I began to wonder out loud what would happen to us if we surrendered.

"We've killed three of their friends, what do you think would happen? You'd never see Penelope again. Now listen, we have to get out of here before they surround us. You start crawling up the hill, and when you hear me fire, get up and run as fast as your legs will carry you until you can't run any farther. I'll follow you if I can, but don't wait for me."

Chapter 31

A Coward

I hugged the ground, keeping the barrel of my weapon raised above the soil. If there was one thing I didn't need, it was a plugged muzzle. Fear gripped me and I wasn't sure I could run, but I jumped up and ran like a scared rabbit when Ananias fired. I ran up and over the hill never looking back.

I ran straight as possible without hitting trees, putting as much space between me and the battle as I could. I picked up speed going downhill, slapped in the face by hanging branches, and tripped twice by tree roots, nearly falling before the ground leveled out. I surmised I must have run four miles; I stopped, leaned against a huge beech tree and looked back. I saw two men, maybe a hundred yards away, headed right at me. I heard thunder and rain pelted down so heavy I could no longer see the men.

I pushed myself to run again. Crossing a rivulet about a mile farther on, I wished I could risk stopping for a drink and a short rest. The rain eased up as quickly as it had begun. I turned to check behind me, and the two men still came. The first stopped, dropped to his knees, and pointed his gun at the other, but didn't shoot. The second man ran at him with a raised tomahawk, and tried to strike a killing blow, but it was blocked by his intended victim's gun. He struck so hard the gun was knocked out of the others hands.

Mesmerized, I watched the two of them circle each other with tomahawks looking for an advantage. One slipped, momentarily off balance; that was all it took. The head of the other's tomahawk buried itself almost out of sight in his skull. The winner struck his adversary twice more, picked up his gun and looked around. Mist rising from the wet ground clouded my vision.

The man searched the ground, head down, walking right at me. It was Ananias. I stepped out to intercept him. "Ananias, it's me. I didn't know if I would ever see you again when I took off."

"Same here. You move fast; I saw you just once ahead of me. Could you see the fight?"

"I did. I hoped it was you, but the fog made it hard to tell. Why didn't you just shoot him? I thought you were going to."

"A misfire, probably because of the rain. I couldn't get it covered fast enough."

"You used your tomahawk like a warrior. You must have practiced a lot."

"Throwing one yes, but never hand to hand. I had no other choice; I thought he was going to kill me. He might have if he hadn't lost his balance when he stepped on my musket.

"Well, tell me what happened when I ran."

"One came on quickly. He had his eyes fastened on the man you shot. He threw himself on him and cried out like he was a brother or close friend. It was fortunate, because it gave me time to reload. I believe he didn't know I was still there, because he stood up and howled. I couldn't miss, and then I ran. Two of them followed me; one was a swift runner, and he was gaining on me. Thank God I can reload while I'm running. When he got close, I knelt down and ended his chase."

"And the second one?"

"I thought I had eluded him, when the rain came down so hard, but I stopped to catch my breath, and there he was, still hanging on."

"He was the one you just killed?"

"Yes. I don't believe there are any more on our trail."

"Do you know where we are, Ananias?"

"Not exactly, but if we keep swinging to the right, we should come to the road we were on this morning."

He was right. We broke out of the woods and in the distance we saw men hobbling and struggling on the road. The defeated remnants of the Tryon County Militia was strung out along the road as far as the eye could see. I was amazed the Indians and the British were not following up and harassing them.

I recognized some men from our regiment as we joined the retreat. I helped a man from the First Regiment. They had the misfortune to be leading the column when they were attacked.

"Hello friend, my name is Jacob Morrissey , Private, Third Regiment. Can I help you walk?"

"I would be much obliged. My name is John Jordan, Private, First Regiment."

"The First was at the head of the column, wasn't it?'"

"Yes, and I was on point with the other advance scouts. I don't know how I survived. The good Lord must have a plan for me."

"Your leg is bleeding pretty badly. Let's stop so I can bandage it. That should help. I've got some buzzard fluff in my pack. You don't want to bleed to death after all you've been through."

We walked a fair distance; a wagon came, picking up the wounded and I got him on board.

"Thank you, Jacob. If you get down to Stone Arabia, look me up."

"I might do that. In the meantime, take care of yourself and heal quickly."

After saying goodbye to the soldier, I looked for Ananias. He had been helping a man who needed a surgeon and I had lost sight of him. We were a sorry looking lot.

It struck me that I had run while the battle raged. I had been scared silly, afraid I would be killed. I wallowed in my shame.

I saw Ananias and I joined him, "I'm feeling mighty low. I've proved myself a coward today."

"What are you talking about?"

"I couldn't be brave today. While our men were being butchered, I was afraid. They stood and fought. I ran."

"Listen to me. Any man who says he wasn't afraid today is either a liar or a fool, perhaps both. You did well. You controlled your fear and stood by my side. Neither of us would have survived alone. You were no more frightened than I was, and there is no other man in our regiment I would rather have at my side in a battle."

I know he wanted to make me feel better, but every time I thought of the men in the ravine fighting for their lives when I ran, I knew I had failed. My worst fear had been realized. I was a coward.

I continued to wonder why the British were not pursuing our defeated army. Many of our men didn't have their guns. The Indians would have had a golden opportunity to kill and scalp the defenseless men.

More wagons arrived, gathering up men who were beyond walking. Some were taken to nearby homes, but the destination for many was Fort Dayton. We traveled to Dayton and then on to home. Ananias had been right, a day of fighting and we would be on our way home.

The morning we left Dayton, men still arrived. General Herkimer, gravely wounded, was alive at his home, but his surgeon feared for his life. I was fit to be tied to be on our way, eager to see Penelope. When we stopped for the night, I brought up the subject of cowardice again. I could not get it out of my head. It clouded the relationship between us.

"Look Jacob, you are no more a coward than I am, but you do me and yourself a great disservice when you continue to look at our actions as less than honorable. We fought our own part of the battle, and we fought it well. Wisdom should never be interpreted as cowardice; that was the reason we walked into that ambush. Now say no more about it.

I thought about it until I fell asleep. I dreamed of the battle. We fought and we ran out of ammunition. We took up our tomahawks, but I looked up and almost on top of us stood an Indian with his musket pointed at my head. I awoke to Ananias shaking me.

Chapter 32

Babies

We crossed the Mohawk and reached my home. No one was outside so we walked to the door, knocked, and entered. "Ananias," screamed Elizabeth, "thank God you are home. We heard about the battle, but no one had seen you or Jacob. We feared for the worst, and I stayed here with Penny waiting for news." She squeezed her husband as much as she could in her condition.

Pen came out of our room holding a small bundle in her arms. "Come and meet your little daughter."

I didn't know exactly how I should embrace her, but she solved it by holding the baby out for me to hold, and kissed me. My body finally relaxed. I had no realization of the stress I had fallen under, even as Ananias and I had walked home. I pulled the blanket open and saw the most perfect, lovely baby I had ever seen. "She is beautiful, and she has so much hair."

"I'm sorry she wasn't a boy."

"Don't be. I always wanted a little girl." We both laughed.

My mother took the opportunity to give me a hug. "Thank goodness you came back alive and all in one piece. When we fought the French, they carried your father back from Carillon, more dead than alive. How bad was it? We heard the militia was nearly wiped out. Is that true?"

"Terrible can't describe it. I've never been so scared before in my life. If it hadn't been for Ananias, I'd probably be lying dead in Oriskany right now. When we left to relieve the fort, we had between 900 and a thousand men. I don't believe more than half escaped. Nightmares. I have nightmares filled with dead men and Indians about to kill me."

Amy had wrapped herself around her father's leg. She looked at me. "Thank you for bringing papa home, Uncle Jacob."

The sudden lump in my throat prevented me from answering. I smiled and nodded.

"Jacob,I am going with Elizabeth and help her out until the baby is born. I'm sure you and Penelope can get by without me for a few days."

"Of course."

We went out to harness Ananias' horse. "Why don't you hook her up to the carriage, it would be a much smoother ride for Elizabeth, and it will give you more room. We can switch things around when it's convenient."

"Thanks, I appreciate it, and I know Elizabeth will too." He threw his arms around me, hugging like the bear he was.

We both rested for a few days. I held our new baby, carried water, and took care of the chores, and I even helped Pen with the cooking. She was doing well, recovering from the ordeal of giving birth. We agreed to name the baby Rebecca, and it seemed to fit her perfectly. She was a happy baby, lively, seldom crying unless hungry or needing a changing. We hadn't heard anything from the Archers, so I decided to take a ride and switch his wagon for the carriage, and I could find out how they were doing.

Pen wanted to go, but decided to wait until I had the carriage, so I went alone, which gave me time to think. I wondered if the battle at Oriskany had done any good, or had so many died for nothing, or worse. Some of our families had lost a father or a son, in some cases both. There was sorrow aplenty. Would we be called out again? Could we even field a fighting force?

Ananias was outside chopping some kindling when I arrived. He put down his axe and waved. He had a smile stretched across his face.

"What's going on? Has Elizabeth had her baby?"

"No, but it looks like it might be today. She has been having some pains, and your mother says it won't be long. I don't really need any kindling, but I had to do something. I was feeling sort of useless."

"At least you are here. I missed out on Rebecca's birth."

"Rebecca? Is that what you named her? I like it."

"We almost named her Abitha, after my grandmother, but finally decided on Rebecca. I came to see how you were doing and switch the wagon for the carriage. Pen would like to come up and it rides so much easier."

"Have you looked at the corn?"

"No, but I was going to do that this week."

"Well, we have a great crop. We will do well if the price of corn doesn't drop, and we were fortunate to have our wheat harvested before we were called out. It could all have been beaten into the mud by the rain. Let's hope the militia will not be needed, at least until our corn is in."

"Should we plant wheat again, now that the war has caught up with us I mean."

"Of course. We can't let a little thing like a war stand in our way. We are going to need food and money no matter what. We've got the seed. We will sow it in early November. Now help me carry in this kindling. Lord knows I cut enough of it. Might last me until October."

Inside, I told mother that Pen wanted to come up in the next day or two. She said, "The baby should be born late today, and Elizabeth is not going to want any visitors right off, so why don't you wait until the day after tomorrow."

I had a cup of coffee with Ananias before we unhooked the wagon and hooked up the carriage. "I'll bring Pen up day after tomorrow."

"I saw some turkeys in the corn today. I think I know where they are roosting. I'll see if I can't rustle up the makings for a turkey dinner when you come."

Chapter 33

Celebrating Good News

Rain erupted in furious outbursts all morning and Pen was loathe to expose Rebecca to the elements, but I did not wish to go alone. We decided to forego the turkey dinner in favor of going the next day when the storm had passed. It worked out well.

The sun bathed us all the way to their cabin, and Ananias met us at the door. "Come in, there is someone I want you to meet."

Elizabeth held a bundle to her breast at the table with mother. "Well, he is still eating, but I'll introduce you to our son, John, when he is full."

I felt someone clutching my leg. "I've got a baby brother, Uncle Jacob. You and Aunt Penny will love him. I do."

I picked her up. "So you are a big sister now? Are you ready to help your mother take care of John?"

"Oh yes. I will sit and hold him while mother works around the cabin. She told me I could, but I have to be very careful."

Pen placed the sleeping Rebecca on the bed and sat down beside her sister. "A boy. You wanted a boy and you have one. How are you feeling?"

"I'm doing fine. It was an easier labor than I had with Amy, and obviously I came through that one. It was a wonderful gift to have Martha here to help me."

"I'm sorry we couldn't get here yesterday, but that rain was awful."

"We didn't expect you would come. No one wants to be out in weather like that" She smiled, "You are forgiven for being wise." She handed John to her sister and covered her breast.

"Oh Elizabeth, he is beautiful!"

"Burp him, or he might spit up. He must be pretty full. All he does is nurse."

I got a look at my new nephew. "I think he looks like you, Ananias."

"I would hope so." He winked and smiled.

"Has there been any news about Fort Schuyler?"

"Not directly, but I heard a large force of New York Continentals are on their way to help."

"Those fellows are real professional soldiers. If anyone can relieve the fort, they will. George told me when he was here after the victory at Trenton they stood toe to toe with the Hessians, as well as any army in Europe could have."

"Hopefully they won't blunder into an ambush like we did."

"Amen to that. He also said General Washington read something to the men before the battle that Thomas Paine had written. He had copied it down and gave me a copy. I can't remember it all, but it started 'These are the times that try men's souls.' I've thought about that a great deal the last few days."

"It says a lot, doesn't it? I'm not sure but what we aren't through being tried. Let's forget about that for now and think about all the corn we are going to harvest."

"I think we should help the Beldock's harvest their crops. Her husband and their oldest son died at Oriskany. They can't possibly do it on their own."

"I'm sure we can get some men together to help them when the time comes. I'll ask around."

Things were quiet in our area, but Fort Schuyler was still under siege, yet somehow holding firm. We heard rumors that St. Leger's efforts to take the fort were growing weaker every day and his Indians were rebelling. The greatest news was that General Benedict Arnold was coming with 3000 Continentals to relieve the fort. We hoped it was true, but one never knew for sure.

Nineteen days after our disastrous battle at Oriskany, Ananias rode into our yard. "Jacob, have you heard the news? The British have abandoned their siege and are in full retreat. They left behind cannons and supplies in their haste to get away and back to Oswego. What say we go to the inn and have a drink to celebrate and wish them good riddance?"

"Let me tell Pen what we are doing and why, and I'll join you. It's time we had good news."

We weren't the only ones in the mood to celebrate; cheers and shouts flowed from the tavern like roaring surf, crashing and subsiding, fueled by jubilation, relief, and spirits. Some who had been at Oriskany, claimed we had killed so many Indians and so weakened the invading force, that we were responsible for the fort's survival. Perhaps our sacrifices weren't for nothing.

Remaining upright in the saddle on my way home was not a given, it was possible we may have over celebrated. At home, I dismounted, and ended up sprawled on the ground. Penelope confirmed my obvious condition. "Jacob Morrissey. You are drunk. Sit down before you fall down." That was the last thing I remembered before I awoke in the morning with Pen staring at me.

"Are you happy now?" She asked.

"Not really. My head hurts and my tongue feels like a rough-cut board."

"You've no one to blame but yourself. Now get up and have some breakfast."

"I'm not hungry."

"You best get some food in your stomach whether you are hungry or not. I hope you don't intend to make a habit out of getting drunk."

"No way, ma'am. I've never been drunk before, and I don't intend to be so in the future."

"Well, your mother said not to be too hard on you. So we will leave it at that. I don't mind if you have a drink or two now and then, but don't go getting drunk. Do you promise?"

"Yes, dear." It was a promise I kept for a long time.

Chapter 34

Is the War Over?

"The fields are white unto harvest, but the workers are few." The verse from Luke 10 popped into my head when I noted how much corn still stood uncut in so many fields. It wasn't the end of the world, but it must have felt like it to the families who had lost loved ones at Oriskany. The sobering thought that it could have been me or Ananias who left family and crops behind, compelled me to help as many as I could, starting with the Beldock's.

Charlie had been a good neighbor, though we were not close, and his son, Benjamin, was strong and affable. Ben had turned sixteen that summer and was sucked into the militia shortly before we went into battle. His father had insisted he stay at home to protect his mother, but he had refused to let his father face the British alone. Charlie was proud of him even though he was ill at ease, because of what lie ahead. He had fought the French. He had faced the horrors of war. He had no delusions. He had warned his son, "War is as close to Hell as any living man can get."

Ananias and I cut and shocked our corn when the kernals were dented, but the stalks still a bit green. The stalks would make better fodder that way, and the corn would still dry for storage. It also gave us more time to help others. A crew of five of us harvested the Beldock corn and left it shocked for the still grieving family to gather the ears on their own. That could be done over a period of time, or they could sell it the way it was.

Our efforts were mirrored over and over again in Tryon County, as men honored those who had fallen. I went home one evening and took out the sheet of paper George had given me and read it again. "These are the times that try men's souls. The summer soldier and the sunshine patriot will, in this crisis, shrink from the service of his country, but he that stands it now, deserves the love and thanks of man and woman." We were loving and thanking those men.

Simon Tarbell came to mind. His aging, arthritic father had explained why his son had not shown up at the regimental muster and the battle. "Simon was in bed with pneumonia and fever. He tried to join the regiment, but I made him stay home, he would only have been a burden."

I had seen Simon at the tavern the day I over indulged in celebration. He looked the picture of health to me. Recalling, *He is a summer soldier or perhaps worse.* Simon and his father were not to be trusted.

The news of Burgoyne's slow and steady advance spread a pall over Tryon County. He expected his huge force of British Regulars, Indians, Canadian Rangers, and loyalists would roll over everything in their path on their way to capture Albany. There was anxious speculation that the Tryon County Militia might yet be called upon to assist in blocking his advance.

The overconfident British general received a wakeup call at the battle of Bennington. Militias from New Hampshire, Massachusetts, and Vermont, stood in the path of a large foraging unit of Hessians and Indians. They killed or captured about 1000 of them. The Indians took especially heavy casualties, but Burgoyne continued on. It was good news for us.

Autumn arrived, adorning the trees with festive reds and yellows, and as their colors brightened and warmed our hearts, so did the news that Burgoyne ran into more difficulty as Continentals in concert with numerous militias harried him. His Indians abandoned him after so many of them had been killed. His unstoppable force grew steadily smaller.

As the leaves reached their peak color, Burgoyne's advance forces met a larger number of Militia and

Continentals. The battle was a deadly one, but lopsided two to one in favor of the Americans. They drove the English soldiers all the way back to Burgoyne's main camp.

A surge of real hope swept over us. It seemed the British certainly must retreat back to Canada and leave us be. We didn't know of course, but the general did not have a retreat in mind. He refused to accept that we surrounded him by an army more than three times his strength and still growing.

The trees were nearly bare when the news came from Saratoga, cannons were discharged in celebration, church bells rang, and taverns across Tryon Country did a brisk business. General Burgoyne had surrendered his entire army and they were now our prisoners.

Ananias showed up at my door. "What do you say we join the celebration in town?"

"No. I don't need another aching head or another dressing down by Pen. But I tell you what; I will have a drink with you to celebrate. Let me get my horse and tell Pen we are going."

On our way, he told me, "Reginald Jones from our regiment, left some time ago to join the men fighting, and he has just returned. He said it was unbelievable how proud he felt when the British were stacking their arms. There is talk that after such a blow to a whole British army, the war is over."

"Do you think so?"

"No I don't. I think it will just make them dig in their heels. I hope I'm wrong, but I believe we are in for it."

"What do you mean?

"I mean one way or another they are going to punish us for such an affront. They will try to grind us into the ground and place the King's yoke around our necks, if they don't stretch them instead. Never let your guard down, even for a minute."

Arriving at Blessed Hope, we tied our horses and I unlocked the house. "Have a seat and I will be right back."

His eyes fell on the bottle. "Hey, that looks like powerful stuff. I hope you don't plan to finish it."

"No. We are just going to toast the victory and sip our drink as we look ahead."

I poured two glasses and handed one to Ananias. "Here's to the victory at Saratoga, and the brave men who fought there.

Ananias had an uncanny assessment of the state of the conflict. We didn't know it at the time, but 1778 was the year the British turned loose their Indian allies and the loyalists to do their worst and ravish Tryon County. The war devolved into a vicious, bloody, no holds barred, series of attacks aimed directly at the civilian population. No one was safe nor exempt, man, woman, nor even child. That included us. I remembered what Ellie's father had said just before he left.

Chapter 35

1778

Fighting continued in the south, but Northern New York quieted after Oriskany and Saratoga. Thankfully, 1777 went out like a lamb. We heard there had been an offer of peace from the British Government, but nothing seemed to come of it. Maybe it was only a hopeful rumor.

Snow fell early and heavy, and the world outside of ours slowed to a crawl. Indians and soldiers would not raid Tryon County while winter held sway. Soldiers went into winter quarters, and the Indians returned to their villages. We had a sleigh, but we seldom went anywhere on good days except for an occasional visit with the Archers.

A four foot deep path led from the cabin to the barn, constantly kept packed down by two trips a day to take care of our animals. The same was true for the short path to the necessary house. As January settled around us we were blessed with a four-day storm that left an additional five feet of snow, and a drift about ten feet high where our paths had been.

I remembered one time while my father was alive, we got such a load of snow that he dug a tunnel between our home and the barn. Somehow it sleeted and rained a bit covering his snow tunnel roof with about an inch of icy crust. It lasted for most of the winter. I didn't know if I would get a crust on top but it took me most of the day to dig our own tunnels to the barn and privy. Pen helped me remove the snow from the inside. It was a lot of work, but it was a break in the monotony and fun to boot.

Trips to see Ananias and Elizabeth came to a halt. There was no way I was going to dig out the sleigh, and we couldn't have gone anywhere with it anyway. The barn was actually warm or at least not cold after the snow had piled up around it. It was also more pungent than usual. Not a bad trade off. The same was true of the necessary house.

We took turns holding the baby and playing with her. Rebecca was easy to care for and happy almost all the time. The rest of us played games, asked riddles, read a lot, got to bed early and slept late, but it was my job to feed the fire during the night. I put on wood anytime I woke up, and the fire never went out. I had time to think when I was up with the fire. I was at peace. The nightmares of Oriskany had faded, and I prayed the war might end soon.

In March, my tunnels collapsed, as temperatures moderated. I started keeping an eye out for Indians. "Pen, anytime you go outside, be sure you look for Indians."

"Have you seen any?"

"No, and I don't know as anyone has, but we can't be too careful."

We didn't know it at the time, but we learned they had been making plans all winter for attacks on our homes. The real war had moved south where Continental soldiers and militia fought standing battles with the British and their Loyalists. We lost more than we won, but the enemy always paid a high price for most of their victories. The continental army had come of age, and it was a force to be reckoned with. We hoped and prayed that the enemy would leave us alone, but Ananias persisted in his gloomy predictions. "This is only the calm before the storm. It will rage about us for as long as the war continues."

Early May brought marvelous news. The French had decided to join us in our war with England. They would send soldiers and equipment, and they would challenge the British Navy. Surely, now our enemy would be hard pressed to fight the French and us. Ananias and I took another trip to Blessed Hope, and I found a bottle of French wine in the Cache. We drank to the health of the French King. We drank to the treaty. We drank to the health of George Washington, and we finished the bottle in tribute to the Continental Army.

"It seems your predictions of the war coming to our doorsteps may have been a little hasty."

"If it were only that easy, Jacob, if only it were that easy. The treaty could just as well cause the English to redouble their efforts to subdue us so they could deal with the French. In the long run, it may well be our salvation, but for right now, I think we must keep our guard up. I hope I am wrong, but I fear for our future."

"Don't be such a doubting Thomas. Why would they risk their lives by attacking us when the war might end at any time?

"The Loyalists and the Indians will never think differently of us. There is nothing to be gained by them in waiting. Possibly if they kill us or drive us out, they might end up with our land in a peace treaty. No. I think this year will be nasty and deadly. We must be prepared. In fact, we should be going home now. The tomahawk could even fall today."

I didn't want to believe him, but I couldn't fault his logic either. "Let's go home, Ananias, I don't feel so much like celebrating anymore."

My battered sense of security proved false. Indians and Loyalists fell on Springfield. Killing three men and wounding several others on May 15th. They burned the barns and houses, carried away food, cattle, and clothing. They killed the cattle and horses they left behind. The little community disappeared.

The militia was called out piecemeal, but we were too late. The enemy had withdrawn. We started to follow their path, but our captain stopped us. "This path is too easy to follow, too plain. I suspect there is an ambush ahead. We will not pleasure them by walking into it."

I have to admit, I was just as well satisfied. Memories of the ambush at Oriskany came flooding back into my mind. We dispersed each unto our own home with a heightened sense of danger.

We learned of scattered attacks on solitary farms. More often than not, a whole family would be wiped out or taken prisoner. Ananias and I discussed what we should do, but the options were few. We could leave now, fight it out if we were attacked, or let ourselves be captured.

Ananias pointed out, "If we leave now, we leave everything, and who knows where we would be safer."

"What about Cobleskill. There are a lot of people there."

"Maybe thirty or forty families, but that's not enough to prevent an attack. I'm not sure what it would take to make the enemy think twice."

"So if we stay, it's fight it out or be captured."

"I think that depends on how many there are. There is no way anyone could resist an attack by ten or more Indians. If you should kill one or two of them, capture might end in death anyway. Don't fight and perhaps you might be captured and taken to Canada. Nothing is certain."

We decided we would stay put and take our chances.

Chapter 36

Premonition

Crops couldn't wait; we started planting just after the attack on Springfield. The weather turned into a farmer's dream, and we were well along when news came of an attack on May 30. Cobleskill felt the wrath of the tomahawk and musket. It was said Joseph Brant and several hundred Indians had led the overzealous defenders into an ambush. About 35 men had been killed, several were captured, and only about ten had escaped with their lives. A new kind of war had come to the Mohawk valley, and we were all in the enemy's sights.

A spirit of helplessness swept over me. There was no place to run, no place that was guaranteed secure, but Ananias had a plan. "We can finish planting soon if we forget about farming the Campbell farm. We can take turns planting, while the other watches for danger. It will take us longer, but it will be at least a little safer."

"I agree. I was going to tell you I had decided I didn't wish to work George's land this year. I don't want to be that far away from my family if Indians show up."

"Elizabeth wants me to stay close as well, besides we will be needed if the men get called out to help in the event of an attack."

"Ananias, Pen and I are interested in you and Elizabeth being Rebecca's God Parents, to take care of her should anything happen to us. What do you say?"

"I don't have to ask Elizabeth, I know she would be more than willing. Would you two consider acting as our children's in return?"

"We were hoping you would do that."

"I will ask, but I am sure she will happily agree."

Once the planting was done, we got together as family at least once a week, alternating who would be the host. It was fun and took our mind off the unpleasant things, at least for a little while. We harvested our wheat in mid-June, including that which we had planted in the fall at Campbell's. Much of it would be sent south to the Continental Army. Our corn was doing well, reaching our knees the first week in July.

Since the massacre at Cobleskill, there had been a number of small attacks throughout the Mohawk Valley north of the river. In some places the people had moved to the nearest fort for protection. Andrustown was an example of that strategy, moving to Fort Herkimer, but from time to time the farmers needed to go back to their farms for planting and harvesting. A small number worked the area on July 18 when a party of Indians attacked. Some men got back to the fort, but three were killed.

Joseph Brant was reported, by Oneida Indians, to be in the area, and it was from his larger band that the smaller raiding parties spread out to torture the land. Numerous, small hit and run raids punctuated August, and we held our breath. Scouts kept a lookout and Oneidas often supplied advance warnings of Indian movements, sometimes even their objectives. But individuals risked their lives every time they ventured out to work.

In September, a large force of Loyalists and Indians raided German Flatts near Andrustown, but the inhabitants were warned of the attack, and almost all of them made it to shelter in Fort Herkimer or Fort Dayton. They destroyed the town, but only three people were said to have perished.

We worked in the corn fields, checking to see when we could start harvesting. "It won't be long now." He said, stripping the husk back on an ear. "Maybe two weeks, maybe less.

"If we don't have any problems with the Indians and Tories, we will be sitting pretty. The price of corn is up, just like the wheat. Maybe we made a mistake not planting corn at Campbell's; after all there haven't been any Indians sighted close by."

"There is no use in thinking about it now, Jacob. We did what we thought best, and because we didn't get hit by Indians should be a reason to rejoice not to gripe about a lost crop."

"I know, but it would have been nice just the same. By the way, it's been some time since I checked their farm. Peter Jones stopped by yesterday and told me he had seen someone at Blessed Hope. I'm concerned; are you interested in riding over with me?"

"It's tempting. Let me know when you are going, and if I'm free I'll go."

We left it that way, but the thought that I should be more concerned about George's home since he depended on me to take care of it, preyed on my mind. I cleaned out the smokehouse, chinked a few spots in the cabin, cleaned the chimney, repaired a chair, and caught up on Pen's to do list. It wasn't hard work, but it took me several days to complete. When I couldn't stand it any longer, I told Pen I was going to get Ananias and check Blessed hope once more before harvest started and bad weather set in.

I rode into his yard and saw the wagon was missing. I went to the door and knocked. No Answer. I decided I would go on my own. On my way back to my place the horse seemed to hobble once or twice. Reaching home, I took the horse to the barn and unsaddled him. I shared the change with Pen. "They weren't home, and Silas has a problem. If I go, I'll have to go alone, and I'll have to walk. Maybe I should stay home."

She gave me a kiss. "Have a good walk, and get it done while it's peaceful here. We'll be waiting for you."

The weight of my rifle grieved my shoulder, and I switched it to the crook of my arm until it began to object as well. I carried it in my hand for some distance. It was a nuisance, but even though there didn't seem to be any Indians around, it was a necessary evil. I nearly jumped out of my skin when a grouse burst out of the bush at the edge of the road. I had never been able to stop jumping when I was surprised by one thundering skyward from nearly under my feet.

How many times had I walked up to this house standing before me? Looking at it, I had a premonition, something was wrong. Had someone broken in? Was someone inside the house? I held my gun at the ready as I approached the door. It was closed and locked. I snuck in quiet as a mouse, I hoped. I listened. Nothing. I walked to the library. Everything seemed in order, the same with the rest of the first floor.

I started up the stairs, my progress announced by the creaking and snapping of each step. If anyone was up there, they knew I was coming. The rooms were fine. They looked just as they had the last time I made the rounds. Relaxing, I walked easily down the stairs and turned back to the library.

As long as I was there, I might just as well have a small brandy to steady my nerves. I opened the hiding place and took the bottle out and set it on the desk. Took a glass and poured about an inch of the golden liquor into it. Sipping it, strolling slowly around a room filled with memories, I began to tremble. Something was wrong. What was it? I put the bottle back in its place and quickly swallowed the remainder of the brandy. I knew what it was. Mr. Campbell's cane with the sterling silver handle was no longer on the desk. It was a mystery, but I did not want to spend a lot of time trying to unravel it at that moment. I wanted to head for home.

I told myself I would come back another day when I could look around more carefully. I put the glass away and walked to the front door. In the distance I saw smoke. Closing and locking the door my premonition returned with a vengeance. I ran down the slate pathway staring at the smoke.

Chapter 37

Flaming Hatred

I realized the smoke might possibly be from our home. I pushed my body to the limit, but I feared the worst. I beat up on myself.

Why didn't I take my horse, he could have stood it? I should never have left them alone. Why did I pick today to go? I should have seen the smoke sooner. Would they be safe?

I knew it was our home halfway there. I couldn't banish the thought "Indians" from my mind, I was terrorized. I hoped against hope, if Indians were responsible, my family might have escaped. They might have been taken prisoner and carried away, but that would be better than being killed.

The ugly plume dissipated long before I reached the top of the little rise above our home. It had disintegrated into ashes; I screamed, their bodies lay sprawled in the yard. I knew the futility, but my weary legs obeyed. I fell on my knees beside them. I could not comprehend what purposely killing women and children had to do with war. It was useless. It was evil.

I retched at the grisly scene, not surprised that the raiders had scalped mother and Penelope, but they had even scalped Rebecca. I dry heaved and lifted her tiny body. A strip of accusing, raw flesh where her beautiful, curly dark hair had been, called forth hot, bitter tears. I hugged her and pressed my cheek against her small bloody head. My tears mingled with her blood; I would have given my life many times over to save her, but I never had the chance.

In all my life, I do not think I ever truly hated anyone, not Simon Tarbell, nor even our enemies at Fort Schuyler, but my mind and my soul changed at that moment. I hated the ones who had done this. I vowed to my precious little girl, my loving wife, and mother, I would not rest until I made our enemies pay a hundred fold.

I told them, "I will hunt down the British, Tories, and the Indians. I will kill them without mercy, I will kill them all and I won't take prisoners. I will take their scalps as they took yours, and I will cut off the Indians fingers and their noses. I will repay them for their barbarity with barbarity and more. They will regret what they have done."

Consumed with an overpowering rage, I was tempted to take their trail and catch them, but I couldn't leave my loved ones lying on the ground. I dug two graves by the flower bed Penelope had started that spring. I buried mother in one and my wife in the other with her arms around Rebecca.

"I will visit you often. You will not be forgotten." I sat on the ground, wrapped my arms around my knees, stared at the fresh earth, and cried. I didn't hear Ananias arrive. I was unaware of his presence until he put his hand on my shoulder.

"Both of them?"

All of them. They killed little Rebecca too."

"I'm so sorry. We were away today. If I had been home perhaps I might have been able to help."

"I'll make them pay, Ananias. I will, you will see. From now on my only interest will be to kill them. Kill as many as I can, wherever I find them. You may have my crops; I don't expect to be here to take care of them."

"Come with me and spend the night with us."

"It won't make any difference. I'm not staying. I will stop from time to time to see them, and when I do, I'll come and say hello to your family."

"It will make a difference to Elizabeth and the children. You are family. Stay this night for them."

I climbed on behind him. His horse accepted the extra weight as she trotted along toward home. We said nothing to one another all the way to their cabin. My chest felt like it would come apart, my head like it was going to explode when I dismounted.

She met us at the door, took one look at me and cried out, "Jacob, what has happened to you?"

I tried to answer, but at best I could only get out a word or two. Ananias helped me get to a chair and I sat down.

She looked at him for an explanation.

"It's bad, Liz. Take the children into the bedroom and pull the curtain."

She came back and he told her, "Indians came. They killed your sister and his mother."

"That's horrible. Is Rebecca safe? Where is she?"

"She is resting with her mother; they killed her too."

Ashen, she said nothing, sitting with her eyes closed. She reached out and gripped my hands, tears flowing. "Stay with us, Jacob. The children would love to have you."

My voice came back in a rush. "Thank you, but no. I have a job to do, a mission. I can't do it here. I must leave in the morning. People need a warning when raiding parties are in their area. We didn't have any warning. If I had any idea they were in danger, I wouldn't have left them alone."

"From the signs I saw, Jacob, there were at least six of them, probably more. If you had been there, you probably would be in the ground with your family."

"Most likely you are right, and I think I would have preferred that, but I'm alive and I have to do something about our tormentors. I'm going."

She looked at her husband and he nodded. "He has some things to work out that he cannot do here. We need to let him go and wish him well. He promised he would return from time to time. Right now, we need to help him get ready for his journey."

Chapter 38

My First Patrol

Ananias gave me a blanket, a pack filled with jerky, parched corn, pemmican, a spare shirt, some hard money, and some advice. "Eat at inns whenever you can, use the pack when you can't. That stuff will last forever. Good luck, and be careful not to walk into a trap."

"Thanks for the supplies. I'll use them sparingly; I may have a long way to go."

"I see you are carrying your tomahawk. Can you throw it? It may save your life one day."

"I can split a squash at thirty paces. That good enough?"

My first stop was fort Dayton. I reported to the commandant, and explained what I planned to do. "I will scout for enemy Indians, but mostly I plan to kill Indians and Loyalists, as well as any poor lost British soldier I might encounter, and I'll bring you back their scalps."

"I want your men to be aware I'm out there. If I come across a group that I can determine where they are headed, I'll come back and give you a warning if I can."

"You will be a valuable asset. You are an official Militia Ranger and Scout as of now. I will see that it is listed as such on your regimental records."

I ate dinner and stayed overnight at the fort. They offered me powder and shot, but I turned them down. "I have plenty, and I plan to use mostly enemy powder and lead while I am out."

I learned how to still-hunt with George, and the deer we shot never knew we were there. I planned to hunt Indians the same way. Hunting the enemy required a lot of sitting, watching, and listening—skills George and I had sharpened. I was out a week before I saw anyone—friend or foe.

My first encounter was not Indians, but a unit of Canadian rangers moving south, probably to join Brant and Butler. There was a single Indian with them, maybe as an interpreter or guide. I watched them go by and dropped in behind them waiting for an opportunity to strike. It arrived midafternoon when two men stopped to take a short break. One of them took off his boots and started rubbing his feet. The other held his nose, said something, and moved out after the group. My intended target pulled his boots back on, stood, and fell forward without making a sound, my tomahawk buried in the back of his skull. I took his powder and shot, and his scalp. I cut a small notch in the tomahawk handle.

I checked his pockets where I found two shillings and his pack where I found some maple sugar and some shot and powder. I hid nearby, watching to see if his friend would come back looking for him. The effort was fruitless, and I left the dead Canadian behind and made a wide loop to the east, hoping to get ahead of the unit and maybe calculate where they were headed.

About an hour before dark, smoke rose from their encampment and I sank to the ground. The light breeze from my right indicated the source of my warning was west of me, but I couldn't see anything. Keeping low, I moved closer. Twenty minutes later, a thin tendril of smoke caught my attention and I saw an Indian sitting by a small fire. I moved carefully, and I got close enough to recognize him as the Mohawk who had been with the Canadians, but his friends were nowhere to be seen. I raised my rifle and drew a bead on my enemy. When I fired, he fell sideways without making a sound. I stayed hidden, listening for any indication of soldiers approaching.

Hearing nothing, I walked over to the dead warrior. He had been cooking a turkey over the fire and it lay sizzling on the coals. I picked it up, brushed off the ashes, and ate my first warm meal in three days. When I had my fill, I dealt with the dead Indian, taking his scalp, throwing his fingers into the fire, and relieving him of his tomahawk. I cut another small notch on my tomahawk's handle. I rested for a couple hours and ate a little more turkey before continuing south. I spent the night hidden in a blow down.

I came across a farm in mid-afternoon the next day and warned the family about the impending raid and sent them to alert their neighbors and get to the nearest fort. The farmer's wife gave me some fresh baked corn meal muffins, which I took and turned back toward the forest. "Wait, aren't you going with us?" She asked.

"No. My job is done here. I am going north to kill the enemy." I wished them good luck and walked back into the woods.

I did a lot of thinking as I searched for my enemy, and I saw several small groups of Indians, but there were always four to eight men. Firing on them would bring about my death as well as some of theirs. There was no way to tell where they were headed. I could deal with two Indians, maybe three if the conditions were right, but beyond that I would pass.

Ten lonely days out, fortune smiled on me. Two Indians walked by me at maybe fifty yards. I was tempted to shoot, but at that distance, a moving target was not a sure thing, so instead, I bided my time and followed. When they made camp for the night, I slipped nearer, their voices covered my approach, allowing me to get close to them, and I waited.

One went to sleep. I could hear him snoring; the second stood guard, blanket around his shoulders and his musket in the crook of his arm. He would be first, but musket or tomahawk? I weighed the two possibilities, decided I would try to take the first one with the hatchet and the second one with my rifle if he woke.

I believed the first man slept on his feet, it was so easy for me to creep right up behind him. I raised my weapon as he swung around, pointed his musket at me and pulled the trigger.

Chapter 39

Brief Encounter

Had the musket not misfired, I would not have been alive to recount the tale, and the two Indians would have lived.

I added two more notches to the handle that night. A full moon forced shafts of light through openings in the green canopy above and gave me all the vision I needed. My search for a safe place to rest ended under a huge blowdown surrounded by blackberry bushes. Confident that I could not be seen by anyone walking by, I slept as soundly as the two Indians I had left behind. However, a turkey gobbling nearby snatched me from my slumber. The woods were still dark, but like a rooster, the birds declared night would soon be gone.

I wanted to get moving, but I knew I needed to resist the urge until I could see well enough to avoid blundering into the enemy. The toms gobbling and the hens clucking in return transported me back to happier times when Ellie had asked me to take her turkey hunting. Her father had agreed she could go, overriding her mother's concern about propriety, after Ellie had said, "Oh mother, we are not going to do anything we shouldn't."

It was the first of several times, and once we even got a turkey for Mrs. Campbell to cook. We huddled together in the cold, predawn air, listening for a bird; I loved every moment of it. We shared hugs and kisses to pass the time, nibbled on scones, and whispered about the future. A mixture of passion and restraint always guided our actions if not our thoughts. I had no intention of damaging my relationship with her mother and father.

I heard the turkeys fly down off their roost and continue their serenade on the ground. It was all interrupted by the sound of a musket shot. I was not alone! A turkey came flying toward me, landing on top of my blowdown, hopping down on the other side and running off into the woods. I could hear indistinct voices and laughter two or three hundred yards away.

I decided to remain hidden and wait to see what would happen.

I don't know if the shooter was an Indian or a loyalist, but in any case, they didn't come in my direction, and I didn't move until the sun was high, and then, cautious—nearly to a fault.

Even with the apparently substantial number of enemy around me, I didn't see any of them that day, and the last hour, I spent finding a reasonably secure spot to spend the night. I would make a habit of that practice.

The next day I took a risk. I saw two loyalists and recognized one. "Charles, hey it's me, Jacob. Man, am I glad to see you."

"Jacob? Jacob Morrissey? I thought you refused to leave with Captain Campbell."

"That's true enough, but my friends started treating me like I were a loyalist. I believe Simon Tarbell turned them against me."

"Who are you with? Where are they?"

"I came down with a bunch of Canadian Rangers. I was supposed to go back home and collect information. I've done that, now I'm headed back to Canada. I had another man with me who wanted to join the Yorker's, but we became separated somehow. I have no idea where he is. Who are you with?"

"The Royal Yorker's of course."

"I'd like to join you, but it's important that I get my information back to Canada. I will try to Join the Royal Yorker's when I get there. Where are you headed for?"

"We are just scouting, but our unit is going to hit our town, gather up a few Loyalists who are waiting for us, kill or capture as many families as we can, and burn down the village."

"That's very cold."

"It's war, Jacob. You know that. It is either them or us; it needs to be us."

"Well, God speed, and God bless King George. I need to be on my way. I hope we will meet again."

"Hey Jacob, one more thing, there is a man who has been killing our men and Indians. Maybe he is the reason your partner is missing. The Indians are calling him the Owl man. He's like a witch or something according to them. It means Death stalks the woods. Sometimes he cuts off Indians' fingers. He must know what he is doing, it really spooks them. Be careful, and keep watch for him."

"But I'm headed north. Surely he isn't up there."

"Don't be too sure. He can be anywhere. He moves like lightening from one place to another, almost like being in two places at once. I've heard he has killed about twenty of our men, some even up by Oswegatchie."

"What does he look like?"

"No one knows. No one has seen him and lived."

"Thanks for the warning. I hadn't heard that. I'll be extra careful."

I started north, but I was eager to turn south as soon as I could and take a warning back to the town and the militia. It sounded like lore had expanded my exploits and the enemy exaggerated them. I couldn't have been more pleased.

It took me two days to get back to town. I went directly to Ananias and I asked him to alert the town and the local militia. "Get Elizabeth and the children to somewhere safer, and make sure everyone knows what's coming. I'm headed for Dayton. I'll alert people along the way."

"I'd give you my horse, but I'll need her to spread the word quickly and move my family."

"I'll be fine. I might find a horse on the way, but I'm a pretty good runner."

I did get a horse from a farmer who had two. "Take her. She has great lungs and she is a powerful runner. She'll get you to Dayton or die trying."

"I won't run her to death. I'll bring her back when this is over."

Having me arrive at the base surprised the commandant. "I thought you were dead. I've been hearing rumors about you from the Oneidas, but they didn't know where you were. You're sure about the information?"

"Yes, I'm sure, and I don't think the attack is very far in the offing."

They rounded up the militia and sent them off in bunches, even as a unit of New York Continental soldiers marched out of the fort to join in the fray.

I was going to join one of the militia groups, but the commandant stopped me. "I am ordering you to stay here in the fort. You are too valuable for me to take a chance of you being killed in the fighting. Eat and get some rest. You have lost some weight since you left. Write up a full report for me. I'll send you back out when I return."

As I started to protest, he waved his finger, "Don't argue with your commandant. Orders are orders; you will stay here."

Chapter 40

Attack Averted

Waiting, wondering, watching for the return of the Continentals, I got precious little rest, but I ate like a horse. The lack of news didn't mean anything, good or bad, but it made it harder to wait doing nothing.

The afternoon the Continentals marched back to the fort was a wonderful day. Some militia had arrived ahead of them, and more were following. The first militia men I talked to shared the events of the past week. "We were ready for them, and they knew they were in trouble when they approached the town. The loyalists had been careful not to alert us by burning cabins and barns, but they were the ones surprised."

"Were many killed or wounded?"

"Not many of us, but twenty-one Tories and nine Indians were killed, and we took seven Tory prisoners, several of them were wounded. The soldiers pushed them at the end of the attack and collected a few more prisoners before breaking off. The enemy had a number wounded that managed to get away. They won't bother us again, at least not right away."

"So you said we didn't have many losses. How many is not many?"

"We had only two men killed and four wounded, none seriously. It was a lopsided victory, and we hammered them good. They came charging and yelling right into excellent range before they realized they'd been had when we opened fire. Are you the fellow that gave us the information about the raid?"

"Yes, that's me. I wish I could have been there with you."

"Don't you worry none. Everyone knows the Colonel ordered you to stay here. Now I'm going to get some vittles, I'm starved."

Even if I never accomplished anything else, I knew I had saved our town, at least for now. I felt spurred to repeat the feat if possible, but first I had a horse to return and a family to pay my respects to. There was little doubt but what it had been what some would call a glorious victory, but I felt very down. I should have been celebrating. Instead I had an ache in my heart, a weight on my back, and a dark place I sank into like quicksand.

****

"Thanks for the horse. It sure made my trip a lot faster and easier."

"You're welcome, but it should be me thanking you instead. You saved the lives of a bunch of good people. The Lord will bless you for that."

"I don't know about the blessing, I am only doing what I feel I must."

"Well, young fellah, if you ever need a horse again, come and see me."

I was dragging when I reached Penelope's flower garden. Someone had kept it weeded and maybe watered too. I knelt and put my hand on the soil. "I told you I would be back. I miss you so much, I miss our little Rebecca, I have made them pay for what they did to you, but the pain doesn't go away. I would give everything I own to have you back here with me. I think about all of you often. I am going to have to leave you again, but God willing, I will return to be with you once more."

I strode along the path to Ananias's home, my heart and mind suffering from the clash of emotions. How I struggled unsuccessfully to put each one in its own separate box. I did manage to shove them aside at the Archers. Both friend and family, they were my link to the real world, to what was important, to sanity in a world gone insane.

"Uncle Jacob!" Amy shouted, grabbing my leg while John toddled unsteadily toward me, lifting his arms, "Unca, Unca.

I picked him up thinking.

Thank God you are safe. You are all safe.

And my life became meaningful again. I couldn't do anything for my mother, Penelope, or Rebecca, but I could try to protect my other family. If it meant others must die, so be it. If it meant that I must die while protecting them, I could accept that.

I picked her up with my other arm. "So how are the two of you doing?"

"We went for a ride, Uncle Jacob. Daddy took all of us to town and we stayed in a block house. There were a lot of people. It was fun."

"And how is my little man doing?"

"He is doing just fine, but he is getting to be a little demanding. He always wants me to hold him or play with him."

"Just be happy you have a little brother. Someday you will be amazed at how grateful you are for him. You won't be able to imagine life without him."

"But I can't imagine it right now."

I laughed and put them down.

"So how was it, Ananias? We sort of turned the tables on them."

"They weren't expecting the welcome that they got, that's for sure. A couple of the loyalists who were killed were from our community. Do you remember John Ferguson?"

"Not really. The only Ferguson I know of was the blacksmith."

"That's it. He was John's father."

"I don't remember him at all."

"How about Charlie McGregor?"

"Yes, I do. I saw him shortly before the attack"

"He was one of the first of the enemy to be killed. The state took over his farm when he went to Canada."

"That's too bad."

"Why do you say that?"

"He was a decent man. Generous and helped his neighbors. I never heard him say a mean thing about anyone.

"I met him and another man in the woods and talked with him. That's how I knew where the attack was heading. I persuaded him I was heading north with information and to join the Royal Yorkers."

"All I can say is we are fortunate to have you on our side. Are you done now?"

"No. I will continue to search for the enemy. When I find them, I will destroy them if possible. I'll be leaving tomorrow morning. Can I get breakfast from you?

"Sure can, and I'll pack you up with jerky, pemmican, corn, and some apples."

"I'm going to get an early start. I want to see if there were any men or warriors who fell behind, either wounded or just slow. They shouldn't be looking for anyone on their back trail by now."

Chapter 41

Vendetta

The sun climbed above the tree line and I finished breakfast. Ananias tried to convince me to stay another day, but I couldn't get our town's raiders out of my mind. "No, I have to go. I know my purpose lies among the chestnuts and oaks, searching out our enemy, not waiting for him to attack us again."

"Then take this coat. It's made from a sheep's skin. The wool inside will keep you warm in the coldest weather. And here is a pair of knitted wool mittens to go with it. At least you won't freeze to death. The winter is coming early. I can feel it."

"Thanks. I will think of you every time I wear them. Now I really have to go."

I stopped by Pen's garden before I left to meet my destiny. "Well I'm off again, Love, but I will see you when I get back. I love you so much and miss you terribly." Picking a flower and sticking it in my hat, I bid them a fond farewell.

I picked up a cold trail, hard to follow with the time that had passed since the attack. I was probably a fool to follow them, but I knew I could watch for other opportunities as I went. Several times, I picked up leaves speckled with darkened blood, and in one place I found a dried circle of blood the size of a plate. There were traces of buzzard feathers in it. Indians used the vultures fluffy under feathers to staunch the flow of blood from wounds. The next day I found a grave, it must have been a Loyalist.

Following the retreating enemy got me nowhere except farther north than I had planned to go, but it gave me an idea. The loyalists and Indians believed I was in their sanctuary as well as near our villages. I would try to confirm that notion. I observed a Mohawk hunting with no one else around, apparently foraging for his village or his warrior group. It was an iffy situation, because he was intent on locating game, and in doing so, he might catch sight of me. I stalked him as I would have a nervous doe. He worked slowly, watching the edge of a bushy area along a creek.

He moved far enough away to allow me to make a wide circle in order to approach the creek about half a mile away, I hid near it, expecting the Indian to pass close by me looking away into the brush.

I jumped when a nearby shot shattered the silence. A deer ran by me bleeding, stumbled and fell just beyond where I was hidden. The Indian came trotting down the buck's blood trail, and stopped beside the beautiful animal, poking its eye with the muzzle of his musket. He grunted, set his musket down and pulled out a knife.

I knew he was mine, because even if another Indian trailed him—which was unlikely—he would most likely think the second shot was to finish off the deer.

I watched the dead Indian for a while before I added another scalp to my collection, and carved another notch on the handle. The Owl man had struck again. It was time to move south, and let the enemy toss and turn in his sleep.

I lost track of time as I moved from one act of retribution to another. The number of Indians and Loyalists increased, and targets became increasingly available. My leather coat resisted the frigid air, but snow would cover the ground soon. I grew weary; a deep need called me home. I encountered two Seneca Indians only a day away from seeing Ananias again. The most vicious Iroquois tribe of all, even the British had difficulty keeping them from murdering civilians. One appeared to be about forty years old, strongly built, and carried a beautiful rifle. The other was young, maybe sixteen, on his first raid, probably dreaming of glory and his first scalp.

I interrupted my journey home long enough to eliminate them. My tracks in the thin snow cover acted like a magnet when they discovered them, drawing them right to me. I shot the older one; the younger recovered from the shock and came charging at me with his tomahawk raised, expecting an easy victory over the white man whose gun was now useless. He became reckless and determined, but I found he lacked the training with his weapon. They were probably a father and son. I studied the bloody young man, my waning hatred ended. The fire was spent, now I would kill my enemy when I had to, but I was no longer driven to search them out.

****

I knocked on their door the next evening. "Ananias, Elizabeth, It's me Jacob."

The kids hugged my legs, Ananias gave me a bear hug, and Elizabeth screamed.

I must have been a sight with my long beard and hair. He said, "I knew it was you for sure when I saw your jacket. Welcome home. We were afraid you might be dead."

"I feel like I am nearly dead. I'm tired, but I have something for you outside. Let me get it."

I handed him the older Indian's rifle. "I thought you might like this. The previous owner no longer needs it. You don't see many Indians with a rifle. Usually they have an old musket at best. It probably belonged to some poor soul he butchered."

"This is a beautiful Rifle. Don't you want it?"

"No. I will keep my old one. It serves me well and I am used to it. I saw quite a number of Indians and loyalists in the last week, but I don't know where they are going."

"An Oneida alerted us; a big raid is aimed at Cherry Valley. He went on to warn them so they would be prepared. He said Brandt and Butler are leading them."

"I wish I had seen either one of them. I would have shot him or both even if it meant I would have been surrounded by Indians and killed."

"Were you successful with your hunt?"

I showed him my tomahawk. "See the notches in the handle. That's how many I laid low."

He counted the notches. "Nineteen, you got nineteen?"

"Actually, I got twenty-one, but I haven't notched my hatchet for the last two yet. May I stay with you tonight?"

"Twenty-one all by yourself? That's amazing. Are you going out next spring again?"

"I won't know until then. I might not; it sort of depends on what happens between now and then. Can I stay?"

"Of course you can. You can stay all winter if you like."

Chapter 42

A deadly attack consumed Cherry Valley in November. We warned them far enough ahead that they should have taken shelter in the fort. A contingent of Continentals garrisoned it, but their commanding officer gave no credence to the report. He refused requests for shelter. It resulted in more than thirty killed, fifteen captured and a dozen wounded. The enemy burned the town and neighboring farms. It saddened me, because it all could have been prevented.

The enemy departed soon after their victory, and we pursued them. Unfortunately, our militia didn't kill many as they withdrew. That was the last major raid in 1778. There were two or three farms burned by scattered groups, but the coming of heavy snows wrote the end to the year's campaigns. I thought it prudent to accept Ananias's willingness to have me stay with them. I would provide some extra protection for them and wouldn't have to make all my own meals.

I felt calm after the events of summer and fall. I amused myself by allowing Amy and John to maul me, reading them stories from the Bible, and helping around the cabin. Ananias and I went hunting for some venison but came home with a turkey instead. It was a welcome change coming up on Christmas time, but a nice deer would have provided more provender.

I used his horse to visit Blessed Hope and found no footprints in the snow. I made a quick check of the inside, and decided to get the brandy. It was only a quarter full after our visits anyway. Christmas and the cold were two good reasons to take it with me.

The children built snow forts and snowmen and enjoyed the opportunity to get outside anytime the weather would let them. Ananias and I stood guard until we shivered like a willow in a light breeze. Then we would call the two of them in, telling them they were going to get frostbitten.

In February, John Jordan came from Stone Arabia for a visit. He claimed he had gotten cabin fever, and when he heard the news of my sad story, he decided to pay his respects. He also wanted to boast about his son who had been born in November, nine days after the Cherry Valley massacre.

"I was so sorry for you, Jacob, when I heard about your family. I remembered how you helped me on the road back to Fort Dayton, and I felt I should come and thank you again and bring our condolences. I could have died at Oriskany, but the Good Lord took pity on me, and then so did you. It was a horrible day. I get chills every time I think about it."

"I do too," I told him. "I had nightmares for quite a while after, but I put all that behind me after my family was killed. I am a different man, but I'm not sure I like what I've become."

"I'm a different man as well. I changed my name, because everyone always said 'Yerdon instead of Yordan' which was really my name, not Jordan. I just got tired of correcting people and trying to remember who I am. Johann George Yerdon will not have that problem. He's only three months old, but he's all boy just like his grandfather."

"He will be just like his father too, I'll wager."

"I reckon. The acorn doesn't fall far from the tree. I only hope I get to see him grow up, and I hope he won't have to fight in any war."

"Amen to that. I have to wonder what this year will bring after all the attacks last year. I can't see where it can be worse than '77 and '78, but we have to be ready."

"Who would like a drink to celebrate?" Ananias asked. "Jacob has been saving the last of a bottle of special brandy for a special occasion. It seems like this one fits."

We had just enough for three small glasses. We nursed it along as we caught up on everything that had happened since Oriskany. Ananias took it upon himself to tell Johann about my crusade after my family was taken from me. "Sit right there, I want to show you something."

He returned with my tomahawk. "I took this off an Indian I shot at Oriskany. He fell right beside us. I handed him the tomahawk and told him it might save his life someday. He has put it to good use since."

Johann took it and ran his fingers over the notches before asking, "You wouldn't be the Owl Man the Indians talk about? They call him *Death Stalks the Woods*."

"Yes I am. I told you I was a different man. I once feared death, now I deal it out and have no fear of it for myself, but I'd rather talk of other things."

We spent the afternoon in more pleasant conversation before he said he was going to the inn for the night.

"We can make room for you here."

"I appreciate that, Ananias, but I'm hoping some more militia friends might be there or the innkeeper may have information about them. I have enjoyed today immensely. Come and see us when you have the chance. Try to do it before Johann the second is plowing furrows."

When he was gone, Ananias said, "Well Jacob, we have finished William's bottle, and didn't even drink to his health."

"He has more, and if he survives the war perhaps we can try to come to a personal peace, and put the ugliness behind us. I could drink to his health then, but not now."

Winter howled into Northern New York and once again provided respite from the depredations of the Indians and Loyalists. Carrying the war to the enemy through snow and zero temperatures did not stir the hearts of Patriots nor Loyalists. But both sides drew up plans, and 1779 would provide ample changes and surprises.

Chapter 43

1779

Small raids broke out in mid-April, and by mid-May, the enemy sent ever increasing forces against us. A band of about twenty loyalists and Indians raided a small community not far from us. They didn't know they had walked into a hornet's nest thanks to an Oneida who gave us warning. A unit of Continentals hidden in homes along with militia, surprised them and put them to flight.

The bell tolled in town, and men gathered ready to assist their neighbors, to kill or capture as many of the raiders as possible as they withdrew. I persuaded the captain to send fifteen men with me to try to intercept their path. I was familiar with the Indian's favorite routes, and we double-timed in our endeavor to catch them.

Arriving at the hollow I felt the raiders would pass through, we set up an ambush.

The Lieutenant, who was in command of our party, asked, "What makes this place different from any number of other places?"

"This is the way they came, and I am sure they will follow the same trail back."

"How do you know they came this way?"

"Because I know them and how they think. This is the shortest escape route, plus I could see signs of a big group passing through here headed south."

"Very well. The Captain told me to listen to your advice. I only hope you are right."

We waited silently, lions ready to pounce. I was first to hear the sound of their approach. They entered the hollow like sheep led to slaughter. I watched a Mohawk and a Loyalist cautiously moving toward me. Remembering my family, I drew a bead on the warrior. Everyone began shooting at the sound of my shot.

A Loyalist officer shouted commands, rallying his men to try to break out. I had reloaded my rifle, bent on bringing an end to his efforts. I had a clear shot, though his back was to me. That made no difference, and when he fell, resistance quickly ended. Most of the surviving Indians were off on their own in different directions. Had it not been for poor shooting by the excited militiamen, few of them would have escaped. Eight Loyalists laid down their arms asking for quarter.

I walked through them to the Indian I had shot. Raising his head by the hair, I completed my routine and moved on to the officer. He had been brave, trying to control the fray and perhaps save his men. Knife in hand, I rolled him over on his back. I dropped my knife; I recognized him. It was Ellie's father. Falling from the pinnacle to the pit, my feelings were scrambled.

"Is there something wrong? The young Lieutenant stood beside me looking at the dead captain. "Are you going to scalp him?"

"No, I'm going to take him home."

"You know him?"

"Yes, he was an honorable man, a good man; unfortunately he chose the wrong side."

"How are you getting him home?"

"I figure a couple of those Yorkers will be happy to do that for me—or I will kill them. I know what choice I would make."

And so it was, we wrapped him in a blanket, and William Campbell returned to Blessed Hope. I had the two prisoners carry him to the top of the hill and place him under the tree. "You, soldier, go down to the barn. You will find a shovel and a pick just inside the door on the left. Bring them up here. Don't run away or I will kill your friend and then the Owl Man will find you."

He blanched and turned a sickly grey, "Aye, sir, I'll get them. Just don't hurt my friend Arty."

Between the two of them, they dug a five foot hole, and then lowered his body into it, still swathed in the blanket. The hole filled quicker than it was opened, and we started down the hill. "What are you going to do with us?" Asked the one called Arty.

"I haven't decided. We are going to the house. We will figure it out there."

"You know we could jump you. You might shoot one of us, but you can't kill us both. Why don't you just let us go?"

"Because you are my prisoners. I can't just let you go, and you might consider I've killed more men with a tomahawk than with a gun."

They went into William's home ahead of me. "Now what?" Arty's friend asked.

"Do either of you boys like Rum?"

They looked at me like I was crazy. "Well do you?"

"Yeah. Sure."

"Then walk to your left and go into that room. It's a library." I followed them in, "Now sit on the floor with your legs spread. You can't get up fast from that position, not before I could kill you. So sit!"

I retrieved a jug of rum and set it on the desk. I got three glasses and poured liquor into each one and sat behind the desk. "Now one at a time, come up and get your glass and sit on the other side of the room."

"Hold it! Before you drink, I want to offer a toast. 'Here's to Captain William Campbell, may he rest in peace.' I think we can all drink to that."

One toast and we drank in silence.

"Would you men like one more?"

"Certainly would, Gov'nor."

"One at a time, come and pour yourself another drink."

"Have you decided what you are going to do with us?"

"Yes, I'm going to take you to the committee and recommend you be paroled if you will take an oath of allegiance to the United States of America."

Why should we do that?

"Because we are going to win, and a friend once told me it's better to be on the winning side. Think about it. If you refuse, the worst that will happen is you will go to prison, but that's better than being dead. Now finish your rum and let's get going."

Chapter 44

George Returns

What was left of my personal war ended when William Campbell died. There was no bile left in me, no desire for revenge, nothing to be proved. I would do my duty; I would even scout, but my desire was to keep everyone safe, not to seek out and kill.

Two things happened in 1779 that benefited us immensely. The British focused on the Southern States, expecting many loyalists to rally around them. They had captured Savannah, Georgia at the end of 1778, and from that solid foothold they pushed north toward South Carolina and west toward Atlanta. The second event was General Sullivan's expedition into the heartland of the Iroquois. The Indians only challenged his invasion of their lands in one unsuccessful battle. The Continental forces spent all summer burning villages, destroying crops and supplies, leaving a barren land behind them in a response to the horrific attacks of 1778.

With the Indians reeling and the British high command turning their attention elsewhere, the year proved to be bearable, not great, but not fraught with continual raids either. I began spending more time at Blessed Hope, sometimes sitting in the shade beside William's grave. Memories of happier days and visions of Ellie would visit me there. I wondered what she might be doing, and if she were happy. I wondered if she had heard about her father. I wondered if I would ever see her again and what that would be like.

I always returned to the Archer's home after a few days at Blessed Hope, and made time to pay my respects to Penelope and Rebecca. The only way I could describe my life was lackluster, day by day without a goal or vision. I harvested our crops with Ananias, but the pleasure and joy it brought me was missing.

Amy asked me, "Are you alright, Uncle Jacob? You always seem so sad."

We planted most of our land to winter wheat. It was Ananias's idea. Wheat prices had been strong for two years and promised to be good for the foreseeable future. A message came to me from our colonel, "Your assistance as a scout is required. Please report to Fort Dayton at your earliest convenience." I said my goodbyes and went back to the trade I had learned so well.

A light blanket of snow grew deeper each day, confirming my service had been completed. I had survived, added two more notches bringing the total to 25, and arrived at Ananias's home, I was more skeleton than man. I needed the winter like our wheat, and I swore I would never go on scout again.

1780 The large wheat crop demanded that we hire help with the harvest. Several young men agreed to work with us, and an abundant crop was gathered, more than we had anticipated. Buyers, eager to purchase, paid us a handsome price, and we in turn gave the young men a bonus over and above their wages. It was a wise move, again suggested by Ananias, because our workers responded, "Be sure and send for us if you need help in the future."

Families returned to their farms; some had cabins, some had only ashes, but they all set about to plant crops. The militia grew stronger as people returned and new settlers came as well. News from the South was mixed, but it sounded like our army took a beating. In the north, Washington and the Continentals drove the British out of New Jersey. The summer in Tryon County, kissed us with sun and bathed us with timely rains, lifting our spirits. Above all else, the absence of enemy activity in our area gave us hope.

On June 27th, I received a message from General Washington himself. I could not fathom why. Breaking the seal, I read, "My dear Mr. Morrissey. Your good friend,

Captain George Campbell, was wounded in our victory at Springfield. His injuries are substantial; dealing with them will take some time. He has requested that he be sent to his home to rest and recover. He should arrive by the 30th of this month. Please take good care of him, and send him back to us when he has fully recovered. He is a brave and valuable officer. Your Servant, George Washington, General of the Armies."

The letter stunned and humbled me. "Ananias. I have to leave. George has been wounded and he will be arriving at any time now. I have to get his home ready for him."

"How serious is it?"

"I don't know, but it must be bad or he wouldn't be coming."

"Don't get ahead of yourself. He may need rest more than anything else, and a good nurse."

"I hope you are right, but I'm not counting on it."

By noon, I had everything in place. I swept through and dusted. If he came that day I would be ready. Ananias knocked on the door at one o'clock, bringing some meat and corn bread. "I'll see about getting you some supplies later today. Elizabeth said she would come to help you out during the day. He hasn't come yet?"

"No, he may not come until tomorrow or the next day, but I want to be ready when he gets here. I don't want to keep you if you have something to do."

"Nope. My time is my own right now."

"Then help me move a bed downstairs. It might make things easier for both of us."

We took the bed apart and moved it piecemeal, reassembled it and made it up with fresh sheets. "That was none too soon," Ananias said. "Soldiers and a wagon just pulled up by the walk."

I guided them in, and the two soldiers eased the litter to the floor, and gently lifted George, placing him in the freshly made bed. They carried his trunk from the wagon and placed it at the foot of the bed. "Be careful of his arm; it is sensitive. Clean the stump and wrap it fresh each morning. He has not been eating well, try to get some food into him. It's the best thing you can do right now."

"I appreciate everything you have done. Would you like something to eat before you go?"

"That's very kind of you, sir, but we need to be on our way back. Everyone says we will be on the march to Virginia soon. We will stop at an inn on our way back and get a meal there."

I pressed money into his hand. "I pray you take this with our thanks."

"We can't take pay for doing our duty."

"I'm not paying you; I am buying your dinner tonight. Eat well, and God speed."

Chapter 45

I Become a Nurse

I sat by his side, day after day, and returned quickly anytime I had to leave him. Sometimes he was lucid, but often he relived a battle.

I killed a chicken for soup. He ate some and even nibbled on a drumstick I set aside, but we struggled every day. He passed his nights in fitful sleep. I slept in cat naps numerous nights. As days passed, we took longer naps, he on his bed and I on a mat beside him.

The army surgeons in New Jersey had amputated his left arm halfway between elbow and shoulder. He complained about burning sharp pains and itching from the stump. It troubled him greatly for a few days, but no infection set in, and the pain slowly subsided. I treated him better than a nurse, but he failed to prosper.

He refused to get out of bed. He struggled, wheezing each breath in and out, and his attitude changed. He said, "Remember, 'Cough' when I'm gone, 'cough' this place and all that's in it will be yours."

"Nonsense. Don't talk that way. You will be up and around in no time."

"I don't feel like I'm getting better. Now this cough, and I'm so tired."

A red flushed face and dark sunken eyes worried me; I put my hand on his forehead. "You have a fever. I'm going for the doctor; I planned to have him check on you today anyway."

"Take your time. I'll be fine while you're gone."

I ran the distance to the village in record time, and thank God, the doctor was there. He grabbed his bag, and we hitched up his buggy. "How long has he been feverish?"

"I noticed it this morning."

"Anything else different? Is he eating?"

"A bird couldn't live on what he eats."

"Anything else?"

"He's been speaking of death."

We came through the door and George coughed several times. Doc stepped closer, opened his bag, and took his patient's temperature. Putting his ear to George's chest, he asked me, "How long has he had this cough?"

"He was coughing day before yesterday. I hadn't noticed it before, but he is having a hard time breathing. I felt a fever today and came directly for you."

"Let's step outside, Jacob."

On the porch, he gave me his diagnosis. "I believe he is developing pneumonia. His fever is strong and he has fluid in his lungs. Set him up in bed, give him all the water he will drink, cool his head with a wet towel, and see if you can get more food into him. His wounds are healing. They will be fine, but the other has me worried."

"How long before he gets over the pneumonia?"

"If he is able to fight it off, a few days and he will be on the mend, if not, he may well be dead by the end of the week, but I'll stop by tomorrow morning and check on him."

I returned to his bedside. "I'm going to sit you up and put a blanket behind you."

"What did the doctor say? I'm going to die aren't I?"

"He said to get you sitting up and give you plenty of water, and get more food into you. He told me when your fever breaks you should be on the mend in a few days."

"I don't feel like I'm going to live. If I die, Jacob, promise me you'll bury me under the old oak on the hill."

"I'll promise, but I'm not going to let you die."

All that day, I swabbed his forehead and the back of his neck.

"You know, Jacob, I would like some oatmeal with some maple syrup. Could you fix that for me?"

That was a good sign. He hadn't asked for anything specifically before. I found the oats and made enough for both of us. The maple syrup was easier to locate, and I poured a liberal amount over each serving. I discovered him sleeping and wheezing. Oatmeal is almost as good cold as it is warm, so I didn't wake him.

I love oatmeal. I set his on the stand and practically gobbled mine down. The earthy taste of the oats and the maple flavor of the syrup brought me a new surge of energy. I decided to wake him because the oatmeal might be just the thing he needed.

He was still hot. "George, wake up. Here is your oatmeal."

"What?"

"Your oatmeal with maple syrup."

"What oatmeal?"

"You asked me for it, and I cooked it special for you."

"I'm not hungry. Just let me sleep."

I took a spoonful from his bowl. "Here, try this. You'll like it, and it will give you energy to fight the fever. Now open your mouth."

He accepted a spoonful, chewed a little and swallowed. "I need some water to help that go down."

I managed to get him to eat four spoonsful. He refused to take any more. He closed his eyes and went back to sleep.

The doctor came back the next morning. Examining his patient, he shook his head. "He's getting worse. I can't do anything more for him. It's out of my hands. He must fight it off himself or he will die. That's all there is to it. Keep trying to get him to eat and drink, and pray the fever breaks. I'll stop by in the morning to see if there is any change."

George suffered a restless night, awake off and on. He grabbed my hand as I swabbed his forehead. "Jacob. The farm is yours. If my family wants to come back, forgive them and take them in."

"The farm is yours not mine."

"It will be yours soon. I dreamed I saw you on the hill by a fresh grave crying, and lowering my body into a hole beside it. Strange. I wonder why there were two graves in my dream."

I hadn't told him about his father. "It was just a dream. We all have dreams."

"Yes, but I could smell the earth and I was dressed in my best uniform without my new boots. I will miss you Jacob. Before I go, there is something I forgot to tell you. Something very important. Ellie is a widow."

"I'm sorry to hear that."

"Don't be."

"Get some rest, you will feel better in the morning, and we will talk about Ellie"

"I think perhaps you are right, I will feel better in the morning."

I slept on the mat beside his bed. He never woke or called for me. About midnight, I awoke, reached up and took his arm. He felt a little cooler. His fever broke, and I finally fell into a mercifully deep sleep.

Chapter 46

I LOST A FRIEND

In the morning, I patted him on the arm to wake him and felt the change. I had encountered it a number of times in the field, when man slips from life into death and the light goes out in his eyes. He is no longer there, only his shell.

I took his arm to check for a pulse I knew I would not find. The stiff arm refused to budge. He didn't need the doctor; he no longer needed anything.

I opened the trunk the orderlies had brought along. A handsome tricorn sat on his dress uniform, beneath which lay a blood stained uniform that had outlived its usefulness. There were some undergarments and hose, a pair of quality boots, a sealed letter addressed to me, and silver coins in a leather pouch.

I opened the letter:

> "Dear Jacob, You have
> been a good friend. If you are
> reading this, you are the new
> owner of Blessed Hope. Make
> sure you get a death

certificate, and have my will read in front of witnesses. If I were unable to give you instructions in regard to my mortal remains, please bury me on the hill under the big oak overlooking Blessed Hope. My purse and the coins are yours, and the buried silver. Don't be foolish and put the new boots on me. They are yours. My old ones will work fine where I am going. Keep my hat as well. I no longer need it. Farewell, my friend."

Another part of my world had crumbled about me. Misery and desolation cloaked me. I disrobed him and washed his corpse. The doctor came in while I completed the task.

He laid his hand on my shoulder. "You did everything you could. I know it may seem foolish, but I need to confirm he has no pulse and that he is not breathing before I can sign a death certificate. George confided in me, saying you were his only heir. That makes you rather well off; he has more wealth than one might think."

"I would rather be destitute and have him still alive instead of gaining by his death."

"I believe you would. I see you have his uniform out. Are you going to bury him in it?"

"Yes, of course, what else would I do with it?"

"Two of us can dress him easier than one. Would you accept my help?"

"I would be much obliged. That's very kind of you."

Even with his empty sleeve, he looked every bit the dashing military figure, except for his old boots. I hung his hat on the hall tree, put his death certificate on the table and pondered my new situation. Ananias arrived, interrupting my thoughts. "Looks like you could use a little help. I met the doctor on my way here. He told me about George. I'm sorry. Where are you going to bury him?"

"Up on the hill beside his father."

"Let's take him up on my horse."

Lifting him over the saddle required but little exertion on our part because he had lost so much weight. We stopped by the mounded earth of his father's grave and placed him beside it while we dug.

Two hours later, we were finished. "Allow me to say a few words, Ananias."

"Lord, I have buried two of my friends on this knoll, a father and a son. They fell in our present war. May they find your mercy and love. Thank you for giving me the chance to know them. May they rest in peace. Amen."

****

The will was read, and as there were no other claimants, at age twenty-one, I became the master of the Campbell Family Home. An alarm took me away once during the summer, but we were too late to catch the raiding party. I completed a number of repairs and updates on the home, and the summer came and went witnessing only a few insignificant raids. Whenever I got too lonely, I would go and spend a day or two with the Archers, but the war dragged on.

My thoughts turned to Ellie after George told me she was a widow. I wondered what she might be doing, if she had remarried, and if she were happy. I had no confidence that I would ever see her again, but the memory of her would not leave my mind. I knew the time had come to visit Penelope again.

I stood by the flower garden, frost damaged flowers shivered in the wind, and I spoke to my family. "Rebecca, I miss you so much. I wish I could hold you again. Mother, I am sorry I was not here to protect you in your hour of need. Penelope, I could not have asked for a better wife. You were beautiful, both inside and out, and I will never forget you, even should I live to be a hundred. Elizabeth told me I need to say goodbye to you and live again, but I'm struggling with that. I have been thinking about Ellie lately. When I do, I feel guilty, but I hope you will understand if I should decide to follow your sister's advice."

Chapter 47

1780-1781

Ananias insisted I stay with them, at least until April, unwilling to allow me to spend the winter alone in my new home.

"Do you think I can't take care of myself, or that I might freeze to death? I'll be fine."

"Elizabeth won't hear of it. She says Penelope would hate your being all alone with no one to love you. We care for you. The children love you. You're family."

"If I stay, it will only be until the weather warms up no matter whether it's April or sometime in February."

'Is Blessed Hope calling you?"

"No, it holds mostly bad memories. I might even sell it and move to Connecticut. I think I could get a position with the solicitors George worked with. Maybe I might join the Continental Army."

"Do what you have to, but wait until spring to do it. Who knows, you might feel differently by then. The war might even be over."

"Sometimes I think the war and the misery is never going to end."

"The war will end. They always do, but misery is a personal thing and it will eat you up if you let it. Come on, stay with us, the kids need you. It will do you good."

"Very well, but only if you agree to let me pay for my keep, and to let me leave when it's time."

"Agreed. I won't argue with you about paying if that makes a difference, but it's not necessary. Elizabeth is going to be so pleased you are staying, and you have just made my life easier."

****

I tapped the maples at Blessed Hope on March 17th, and for several weeks, we reversed our living situation. I insisted they come and help with the sugaring. It brought some happiness back into the home. Elizabeth cooked and found other things she thought needed doing. The kids explored the house which seemed huge to them compared to their home. The sap ran well, keeping us busy emptying buckets, and at the same time we kept the sap boiling. Ananias and I gathered while Elizabeth kept track of the cauldron. We used the horse and sleigh for bringing the sap to be boiled, everything else was plain hard work, but the rewards justified the means. Soon we were eating pancakes with new maple syrup.

"This is a good season. We will have syrup and all the sugar we need for the year. If the weather doesn't get too warm, and the trees don't bud, we will have some to sell as well. It's going to be a grand year."

"We helped make syrup, Jacob, but the real treat was working together as a team. The snow hasn't disappeared under the evergreens, why don't we make some jack wax for John and Amy before it's gone?"

"For the children, eh? Help me scoop up some clean snow, and Elizabeth can boil down some syrup. I could use some jack wax myself, but I don't have any dill pickles to go with it."

"What are you talking about?"

"Dill pickles. Certainly you have eaten them with jack wax?"

"Never. Never even heard of such a thing, but we have some pickles left. I can go fetch some."

"No, don't bother. I can do without them."

"I'll go after them. I want to see you eat them with the maple."

He left riding bareback. That day he learned something new. The sour pickles cut the sweetness of the syrup, making it that much more enjoyable, at least to me.

"Well, I have to admit I didn't believe your story, but there is something to say about the combination. It's not my favorite thing though."

"Give it time, it will grow on you."

"Moss might too, but it would take a long time."

****

My adopted family returned to their home in mid-April, a week or so after the sugar season ended. They took 30 pounds of sugar and 8 gallons of syrup with them. We set aside an equal amount for sale, and I kept 15 pounds of sugar and 3 gallons of syrup. I insisted on the unequal distribution to quell their hesitation to accept the lion's share.

"I don't need more than what I'm keeping for myself. Besides, you never know when I might drop in for a stack of pancakes or a hasty pudding. I expect I will help you with your share."

"I will hold you to that. We will be planting oats in a few days and we will talk about it."

Raids of 1780 had seemed insignificant to me, because I misjudged their importance. They had been a sign, not of the enemy losing heart, but of their growing strength and audacity. 1781 had started as a sweet year, but it would explode in Tryon County. The largest numbers of invaders since Oriskany ravaged us and renewed the bitterness in my heart. We were harvesting oats when a militiaman arrived from Fort Dayton. More than 300 Tories and Indians had attacked Argusville and Currytown on July 10th. Colonel Marius Willett had engaged them with about one third their numbers, and his strategy and the bravery of the Militia, devastated the enemy. They turned tail and ran for Canada, but they left more than 40 dead behind them and a number of seriously wounded.

"It sounds like a victory any way you cut it, Ananias."

"What I'm saying is we need to be watchful. If there were that many at Sharon Springs, some of them could be headed here. I doubt that they went all the way to Canada with their tail between their legs."

"We can bring extra ammunition with us just in case. We will be finished with the oats soon. Then we can stay close to home."

"I don't know why, Jacob, but I have a bad feeling about this. Let's work faster. I'll get Elizabeth and the children to help. At least we won't have to worry about something happening to them while we are working."

"That's a good idea. Not only will we have some extra hands, but we will have more eyes."

From reports, there were Indians skulking around in the woods all the way from Fort Schuyler to Lake Champlain. Of course many of them were figments of people's imaginations, but the danger was real. For a while, I stayed with the Archers. Ananias and I would take turns standing watch at night. Then on August 10th, everything changed.

I watched in frustration as Ananias packed up. "They didn't send for me. Why you?"

"Just my turn, I guess. They have been selecting men to act as scouts. Indian activity has picked up, and Willett wants to know where they are and how many there are. He doesn't have enough scouts he can send out to do the job."

"I'm a good scout. I've proven that. How come they didn't send for me?"

"Who knows? I'm just happy you will be here taking care of everyone."

"At least let us know what you are doing, how you're doing. Send us a letter whenever you get a chance."

"I'll do that."

I watched him ride away. The children waved, standing beside their mother. I had never worried about him before, but this time I couldn't help it.

Chapter 48

Ananias 1781

"August 12, 1781.

Dear family, here I am twiddling my thumbs, but the colonel is assembling a team even as I write. I volunteered, and we'll be off in the evening. We will leave Dayton in the dark so the enemy will be unaware of our departure, and we can be in the woods long before light. We were told to take three days rations. I will write when I get back to the fort. Love, Ananias"

Elizabeth wrote him a short letter, and I did the same. With any luck and good weather they should be there to welcome him.

"August 16, 1781.

Dear family, Thank you for your letters. The Colonel's intelligence proved accurate. We discovered a recently used trail at daybreak and followed it all day. Shortly before dark, our Sargent heard voices ahead.

We discovered six Indians and two rangers. We killed the two rangers and five of the Indians. One escaped. It was over in just a few minutes. We suffered no casualties. I will get two days rest before we go out again. Love, Ananias"

"August 19, 1781.

Dear Ananias, Thank you for letting us know you are well. John and Amy each wrote a note to you. As you can see, I included them. Everything going well here. Be careful. Love, Liz."

"August 22, 1781.

Dear family. We were out four days. We saw signs of the enemy, but couldn't make contact. On our way back in we caught a Tory and brought him to the Colonel for questioning. He was rather insolent until I took out my scalping knife and had his arms tied behind his back.

I warned him, 'a man doesn't have to be dead to be scalped, and if you don't quit your foolishness and cooperate, you will find out.' He became a cooperative prisoner. I asked him if he knew Ellie Campbell, but he had no idea who she is. Thanks for the children's messages. That's all the news for now. Love, Ananias."

No new letters arrived until September 4th.

"September 1, 1781.

Dear Family. I have had but little time to write, but I am being assigned as a lead scout for a company under a Lieutenant Solomon Woodward. The unit should arrive in a few days, and I have heard good things about the officer. The enemy grows in numbers and are becoming bolder. We need to know how many there are. Our Tory guest said there were 900 men. I think he is exaggerating. Love, Ananias."

"September 7, 1781.

Dear Family. We are leaving very soon to scout along West Canada Creek. There have been reports of enemy activity in the area. I heard that the Lieutenant can be very rash and impulsive. Tell you all about our adventure when I get back. Love, Ananias.

****

I will tell you the story as I heard it. Lieutenant Woodword led 46 men and six Oneidas out of Fort Dayton early in the morning of September 7 to scout along West Canada Creek. They had gone only two or three miles from the fort when they struck a fresh trail left by a sizeable force. There was a discussion about whether they should send a runner back to the fort for reinforcements, but the Lieutenant said if they waited, the Indians would be gone. Ananias and the other scouts followed their trail, but ended up walking into an ambush. Twenty-two men were killed. Among them were Lieutenant Solomon Woodward and Private Ananias Archer.

Elizabeth didn't want to believe it until we received an official notice of his death from Colonel Marinus Willett, Commander, Tryon County Militia. I was angry once more; she was devastated.

"What will I do, Jacob?

"You will get through this. I will see that you have the things you need; you will not have to go without."

"I can't farm the land, run the house, and take care of the children."

"I will tend to part of the land, but you could hire someone to take care of the rest. You would still have an income."

"I could go and stay with my father and mother, but I would hate to leave my home."

"Why don't you take a few days to think about what you want to do? You don't have to make any decisions right now. I'll stop by every day to check on you if you like."

"Thank you, I believe I would like that. At least for a while."

I had a problem. I had committed to stopping to see the Archer's each day, but I wanted to put my tomahawk and scalping knife to work once more. I wanted to terrorize the enemy; I wanted to give him nightmares, I wanted to kill them all. Then there was the harvest to bring in, it took priority over my desire for revenge.

My daily visit had evolved into a regular breakfast at the Archers. Amy and John appeared to have put the death of their father behind them. One morning, Elizabeth said, "Would you consider passing the winter with us? We would love to have you."

"Say yes, Uncle Jacob, say yes." The children shouted and danced around us.

"What would people say, you being a widow and a single man living with you?"

"Nothing more than they are already saying. You can sleep on the bed near the fire."

"I don't know. I don't want to be responsible for sullying your good name, and hurting your chances to find a new husband."

"Let me worry about that. You can be my hired man. Will you stay?"

Chapter 49

1781–1782

I brought in the crops, thinking about what she had said, and she and the children assisted me with the harvest. I hired a couple workers as well, and we finished on October 15th. That night she asked me, "Have you made any decision about spending the winter?"

"I have. I would be pleased to spend the winter with you and the children."

"That's wonderful. They will be so happy, especially since their father is gone."

A little over a month after Ananias died we got word that Washington and the French Navy had a British army cornered in Virginia, and pounded the daylights out of them. I paid the young men who worked for us and bought them a drink at the inn. The inn keeper asked "Have you heard the latest news?"

"What news would that be?"

"General Cornwallis has surrendered his entire army to Washington at Yorktown. Everyone is saying it means peace. The war is over. They can't fight the French and us too."

****

The children were accustomed to seeing me in the house during the winter, but I was uncomfortable spending it with Ananias' widow. The food was better than I remembered, the children absorbed me in their games, and Elizabeth did my laundry and any mending that needed doing. It was much preferable to living alone.

I stopped by Blessed Hope from time to time on good days. Once I stopped by the tavern to learn if there was any news about a peace.

"Jacob, I haven't seen you lately. I heard you were living at the Archer's."

"That's true enough, I am. Have you heard any news about the peace, or are we still at war?"

"Nothing at all. How is she?"

"How is who?"

"The widow Archer, is she all the woman she appears to be?"

A voice came from the back of the room. "Is she with child yet?"

It was Simon Tarbell, and he sounded like he had been celebrating more than a little too much. "Watch your mouth, Simon. There's nothing going on between Elizabeth and me."

"You expect us to believe that? You are probably in bed with her every night. Is she as good as Ellie was?"

"Simon, I'll let that pass; you are drunk, but if I ever hear such talk from you again, drunk or not, you will become another notch on my tomahawk."

I stormed out of the tavern before my anger could get the best of me. I feared this result of my stay. I decided I had to let Elizabeth know what was said. Perhaps it would be best if I moved back to Blessed Hope.

"I'm back." I announced coming through the door.

"That took you a while. Everything in order at the house?"

"Yes, everything is fine. I stopped at the inn to see if there was any news about a peace."

"And is there?"

"No, nothing. We may be in for another year of war. What a waste! There is something else I have to tell you. You are not going to like it."

"You aren't being called to go on a scout are you?"

"It's something worse than that."

"What could be worse than that?"

I told her about the conversation at the tavern. "I could have killed Tarbell."

"He's a fool, and he was drunk. You would gain nothing by killing him. The barkeep can always be relied on for juicy gossip, and if people are talking, then shame on them and their evil thoughts."

"I probably should move out."

"You will do no such thing! If I can ignore such ridicule, you should be able to as well. Are you unhappy here?"

"No, not at all."

"Then let the others be damned, every one of them. I care not what they say."

That was the end of it. I stayed and ignored the looks and snickers when I was in town. I was sure Ananias would have approved, and it felt like I left home when I returned to Blessed Hope in the spring. Elizabeth made me promise I would continue to come for breakfast and an occasional dinner.

****

Peace might be coming, but the Indians hadn't heard. They raided on a small scale, burning farms, killing a farmer now and then, or capturing and taking prisoners back to Canada.

We weren't attacked by British regulars or loyalists. England sent a new Commanding General to America with instructions to suspend all aggressive action. The regulars were mostly shipped out of the area to where there was more need for their services. It wasn't peace, but it was as close as we were going to get.

After oat planting, news came that confirmed they held peace talks. Parliament lost interest in subduing us and voted to end the war. That certainly explained the complete absence of British troops in Tryon County, but the Indians were not ready to make peace with us. Their raids became less frequent and parties of three or four braves was the norm, no more large attacks, but farmers had become less vigilant, less cautious, and people still died.

"Elizabeth, I would like you and the children to come to my home where I can protect you better."

She smiled. "What will your neighbors think?"

"It doesn't matter what they think as long as you are all safe."

"I will consider it, but you don't have to have us underfoot all the time."

"You won't be. I have gotten spoiled from living with you all winter, and I wonder if I can get by on my own anymore."

"I see. Are you telling me you want someone to cook your meals, take care of your clothes, and keep the house neat and clean?"

"It sounds like an imposition when you say it like that."

"It sounds to me like you are looking for a maid or a wife. Are you?"

"I don't want a maid, and while there is still a war going on, I'm not sure if it's fair to take a wife."

"Honestly, Jacob. Do you think it would be any less painful to me if something happened to you now, than if we were married?"

Chapter 50

SUMMER 1782

She agreed to join me at Blessed Hope, but her demeanor changed. She performed the tasks around the house more like she had to than wanted to. She said nothing about marriage, but her eyes followed me, sometimes angry, sometimes hungry. The good times we had at her cabin weren't forgotten, but they were overshadowed by the impasse we were enduring. We hadn't planned it, we didn't want it, but it consumed us all the same.

"Jacob, I don't think this is going to work out. I'm going to take the children and go home."

"I wish you wouldn't do that."

"Why?"

"Because I don't want you and Amy and John living by yourselves. I can take better care of you here. You'll be safer."

"Who asked you to take care of us?"

"Ananias. We had an agreement."

"Is that so? He never mentioned it to me."

"It was an agreement to watch out for the other's family in case one of us died."

"I thought you were just being kind to me and the children. I didn't know you had to be."

"Elizabeth, stop this. You know that's not the reason. Why are you acting like this?"

"Because I love you. There, I've said it. I thought perhaps we might get married at some point, but everything was just a fantasy. You are so inhibited by your thoughts of your precious Ellie, that you have no room for anyone else in your heart. I can't fight that. I'm going home."

"Are you sure about this? You would be safer here."

"The war is over. We don't have to be watching over our shoulder every minute. I can protect my family."

"But the war isn't over. The Indians haven't forgotten Sullivan's army, and they are taking their venom out on us. People are still dying."

"I'll be safe enough, Jacob."

"Will you stay a few more days and think about it? I truly wish you would stay, and not because of Ananias. I would have watched out for you anyway."

"Do you love me?"

"I've thought about you a lot. I am fond of you, and I might very well come to love you."

She turned away. "When that day arrives, come and get me. I'll be ready, but for now, take me home."

"After I take you home, may I still stop by and see you and the children?"

"Of course you can. We are still good friends even if you don't love me."

****

I stopped by often, especially when I was working nearby. I hired a reliable man from the village to help with the farm when he was needed. There wasn't much for him to do in August, but I told him we would be busy from mid-September through October.

The corn grew tall and the ears were full and lengthy. The fields behind the Archer home were lush, already towering over my head. Elizabeth and I stood outside surveying the field. "I don't believe I have ever seen a better field of corn, I wouldn't be surprised if we get 120 bushel an acre this year."

"Do you really think so, Jacob? I don't remember ever getting more than ninety in a good year."

"Come over to the corn with me. See this stalk. It has two ears, which isn't unheard of; although, most stalks will have one. What is unusual is both ears look fully formed. Usually the second ear does not produce much corn. If even half the crop is like this, we will still have a bumper crop."

"That's wonderful. I can hardly believe it."

"The price will probably fall, because there will be so much."

"Well it still sounds like a blessing. Would you like to come for dinner Thursday? I've got some old hens that aren't laying and they aren't sitting either. I'm going to turn them into chicken and biscuits."

"I wouldn't miss it. I'll be over in the early afternoon and play with the children for a while if that's agreeable."

"That would be fine. They will love it."

On my way to a chicken dinner, I stopped to pay my respects to my family. I could see that Elizabeth had been keeping the flower bed weeded. I was pleased; she didn't have to do that. Grass filled in much of the wagon trail between there and my destination. I allowed the horse to take his time, the sun sapped his energy, and I was in no rush.

I rounded the last bend, and the cabin stood before me. The door was open, but I didn't see anyone outside, and I didn't hear the children. They should have been outside waiting for me. They knew I was coming.

Something was wrong. I fastened the horse to the post and walked to the house, cocked pistol in hand. Spilled flour and parched corn lay on the ground. I peeked inside past the edge of the door. It looked like a bear had ransacked the cabin, spreading ruin in his path.

I entered and looked to see if the culprit was still inside. Broken furniture, some unfolded cloth, and the overturned table forced me to move closer to the fireplace. From there I saw Elizabeth lying on the floor. I had seen ghastly results of battles and Indian raids, but nothing ever prepares a man to see his loved ones butchered, and surrounded in a pool of their own blood.

I checked her, but she was obviously dead, and she hadn't been killed by a hungry bear. They never scalp their victims. I feared what I might find, but I moved on and checked the bedroom, expecting to see the children. Relief flooded over me when I didn't find them.

I took a closer look at Elizabeth. It was apparent she had died fighting for her life and children. She had several knife and tomahawk wounds on her arms. She had been struck in the head twice by the tomahawk. There was nothing I could do for her. She had been murdered and scalped, but Amy and John weren't inside the house. I was sure they had been taken captive and were on their way to

Canada. I thought with my horse I might be able to follow their trail and catch up with them.

I walked back outside, ready to leave in pursuit of the Indians. As an afterthought, I shouted, "Amy, John, where are you?" I called several times hoping against hope that they might be hiding nearby.

I gave up hope, and I mounted my horse ready to leave, but I heard something from behind the cabin. I listened, "Uncle Jacob, is that you? Uncle Jacob." I rode around the cabin and the two of them stepped out of the corn field.

"Are the Indians gone? Is mother alive? She told us to hide in the corn field and not come out until someone called our names. We heard a shot, but we didn't hear anyone call until you did. We could hear the Indians looking in the corn for us. We were scared and kept real quiet."

"You did well. Your mother would have been proud of you. Do you know how many Indians there were?"

"Mother told us there were three Indians coming, and we should hide in the corn. We didn't see them. Is mother dead?"

"Yes she is. I want you to climb up here with me. Amy, take my hand you can sit in front of me. John, you can sit behind me. Wrap your arms around me. I won't ride too fast, but I'm going to take you to town and get some men to help me go after the Indians. Now hold on tight."

I left the children with the Doctor and his wife. It didn't take long to round up half a dozen men to join me, and the trail wasn't hard to follow because one of them bled. I knew Elizabeth had gone down fighting. If that slowed them down, we might have a chance of catching up with them.

Chapter 51

My New Family

We found the trail. Blood and drag marks made that simple. Obviously, one of them was wounded. The discovery encouraged us and spurred our efforts.

"We are going to catch them, I'd bet my farm on it, but even if one dies we will be closer than we would have been."

"If one dies and they don't carry him, we will never catch them, Thomas, unless we are lucky.

"What do you think happened to the wounded one?"

"My guess is Elizabeth shot him. That might be why they killed her instead of hauling her away with them."

"Why do you think they didn't look harder for the children?"

"Probably a couple things. They didn't want to stay around too long and be discovered, and they had a wounded friend they needed to care for."

"Look Ananias, more blood."

"He is getting weak. They are carrying him now; there are no more drag marks. That will speed them up, but it will tire them too."

We kept on until dusk without catching sight of our quarry. It was unlikely they would move in the dark, and they wouldn't expect anyone following them would either.

"Make a cold camp and get some rest men. I am going on ahead tonight to scout. Follow their trail as soon as it gets light enough to see." Push hard in the morning, I don't think they are too far ahead, but they may yet escape if we come upon them at night."

"What if you find them or they see you?"

"I'm going to get around them if I can. If you hear shots in the morning, come as fast as you can. I'll see you then either way."

I had traveled about three hours when I heard someone groan. I had to be close, maybe too close. I took my time to ease away from there and move ahead of them. I settled down to wait for morning, peering into the darkness.

Morning came with no sign of them. I had guessed wrong. Now I would have to either wait for the rest of the men, or try to pick up the trail alone. I decided to wait. The sun was well up when I heard shots. Alerted, I searched for movement. An Indian appeared with a gun and he watched over his shoulder for pursuers. He was looking for danger in the wrong direction.

Twenty minutes later I saw them and heard, "There's Jacob. Hey Jacob. We're here."

"Did you get the other two?"

"We shot one. The wounded one was dead already. I see you got the other one."

"Yes, you drove him right into me."

"Wonder which one of them killed Elizabeth?"

"This one."

"How do you know?"

I held up the rifle I had given to Ananias. "This was her gun. It only makes sense; he wouldn't have had it if the other brave had shot her."

Two of the men helped me bury her when we got back. We took her down the trail and put her to rest next to her sister. I wondered if I were accursed. Everyone I held dear had been taken from me. Everyone except Amy and John. I went back to town and collected them; we were now the family.

****

1783

I heard so many peace rumors that I wondered if it would ever come or would we just bumble along in a state of quasi war until we were exhausted. It was true that peace talks had started not long after Elizabeth's murder. Indian raids had diminished to mosquito bites, and British troops abandoned one Southern port city after another, but there was no treaty.

"Uncle Jacob, can we go fishing?"

"Maybe this afternoon. We still have some work to do in the field. Your father was a good farmer, and I vow you will be also. I need your help today."

"Are we going to live with you always?"

"I certainly hope so. Your grandfather and grandmother are not able to take you, so that leaves only me, right?"

"Amy is afraid you will have someone else take care of us, that you would send us away."

"I'll never send you away. She doesn't have to worry about that."

"I told her that, but she worries just the same. Can we go fishing?"

"I guess the work can wait. You and Amy get your poles and we will see if we can catch fish for dinner."

The fishing was good. I spent time baiting Amy's hook and taking her fish off. John had learned to do it himself; I don't think Amy wanted to learn, but it gave me a good chance to talk with her.

"Your brother tells me you think I might send you away. What could possibly give you that idea?"

"Well, sometimes you have to go away for a long time. We can't stay here alone, so you would have to send us to live with someone else."

I put my arm around her and kissed her cheek. "Amy, I will never leave you. I will not go away again, I promise you."

"And you'll never send us away, ever, no matter what?"

"No matter what. You two are my little boy and girl now, and that's that."

"She hugged me, saying nothing for a time, then she kissed me. "I love you, Uncle Jacob."

I wanted to tell them they could call me father, but it wasn't the time. "Then how about learning to put your own worms on your hook?"

"Oh, Uncle Jacob, I can't do that. They are all squirmy and dirty."

We had fish for dinner that night, and John learned how to clean them. Amy insisted she wanted to help cook them. Learning to bait her own hook could wait—forever as far as I cared—it was a delicious meal.

Chapter 52

PEACE

Church bells shouted the news far and wide, musket shots rent the air, and the town cannon fired twenty-one times. Men crowded into the tavern, laughing, crying, and drinking. There would be headaches tomorrow, but today was a day for celebration. We had won, we were a new nation, and we basked in the realization there would be no more raids, no more British soldiers, and no more taxes from parliament. We were free.

I spent most of the next day with my children taking care of Penelope's flower bed instead of nursing a headache. I was happy that peace had finally come, and I could get back to farming and learning how to be a father, but bittersweet memories clouded my world. Yellows and purples of fall flowers greeted us and stood watch over graves. I pictured the ones buried there and grieved anew.

"What's the matter, Uncle Jacob? You look so sad."

"I was just thinking about your mother, your cousin Rebecca, your aunt Penelope, and my mother. I buried each one of them here. Your Aunt planted the flowers, Amy."

"They are beautiful like the ones at your home."

"Yes they are. Another person planted those, Mrs. Campbell. It was their home and her garden. Now they are yours."

"Really? Is she buried there?"

"No. She may even be alive for all I know."

"Why did she go away?"

"It's a long story."

"Will you tell us?"

"Maybe someday, parts of it anyway."

"Was she pretty?"

"Who?"

"Mrs. Campbell."

"Yes she was pretty, but not as pretty as your mother or Aunt Penelope."

We pulled the last of the weeds and climbed back into the carriage. In sight of Blessed Hope, Amy asked, "Will she come back, Uncle Jacob?"

I flinched and thought of Ellie, but I realized she must be asking about Mrs. Campbell."

"I don't know. Her son asked me to allow her to live here if she came back. If she does come, I will take her in. She could be like another mother for you two."

****

I was amazed how quickly things went back to normal after the war. I hung Ananias' Rifle over the mantle and put my tomahawk away in George's trunk. The rifle reminded me of family, the hatchet only of war and the lives I had taken. At first, I put it on the mantle with the rifle, but I couldn't bear the accusing look it gave me.

The children helped with the harvest that fall, along with the man we had hired to help Elizabeth. He lived in the Archer home as a tenant and paid some of his rent by helping me. It worked out well, because I had more land now than I could possibly work, and he saved money on his tenant expenses. I put all the hard cash into a bank for the children and hid it in the secret library compartment.

I taught the children to read and write using the Bible as my mother had done for me. I was not a teacher, but I managed, and thank the Lord I had a pair of prodigies when it came to recognizing words. I was surprised when John got the hang of it first and he helped his sister.

"What are you doing there, John?"

"I'm writing down what we did today. I'm keeping track of everything."

"And why are you doing that?"

"Because I don't want to forget."

"Do you know what that's called?"

"Writing?"

"Yes, it's writing, but you are keeping a journal, a record of each day's events."

"I want to write down what I remember about mother and father. Would that be all right?"

"It would be more than that; you would be creating a treasure."

We spent the winter reading and writing, and before spring came, we were learning numbers and counting to one hundred.

"You two have done so well, I will teach you how to add numbers together before it comes time to plant. I swear you are probably the smartest youngsters in all of Tryon County."

"It's fun, Uncle Jacob, and you are probably the smartest man in all of Tryon County."

"That makes us a pretty smart family, but don't go telling people that we are so smart. Some people wouldn't like that. It will be our secret."

"Uncle Jacob, are you going to find a wife?"

"I don't know. Perhaps. Why?"

"If you do, will she be our mother?"

"I suppose so, if you would like her to be."

"And if she is, wouldn't that make you our father?"

"Would you like me to be your father?"

"Well you play with us like a father, you love us like a father, you teach us like a father, why shouldn't we call you father?"

"Well, I'm not your father. We will talk about it later."

****

1784

The letter came that summer. It was addressed to George Campbell, Blessed Hope, Tryon County. It was worn and well-traveled, but eventually someone had recognized the name and sent it in the right direction. "We knew

George was dead, but you inherited his estate, so we brought it to you."

My hands trembled, my eyes fixed on the name of the sender, "Mrs. Elspeth Campbell Fitch."

"Forgive me George, but I'm going to read your mail. I'm sure you won't mind." I opened the envelope, unfolded the letter, and began to read.

"Dearest George, I hope this letter finds you well. You may have heard that father was killed in the war. We had hoped he had just been captured, but his men were sure he had been killed, and so it proved; although, they never found his body. Mother and I are well.

I am going to visit you. My coach is scheduled to arrive in the early afternoon on June 17th. Please come and pick me up. I am so looking forward to seeing our home again.

Your loving sister, Ellie."

She was arriving in two days!

The children observed me reading the letter, and John asked, "Who is it from?"

"An old and dear friend, someone I knew so long ago."

"Who is he?"

"It's not a he, it's a woman. She is coming to visit us in two days. We need to get this place spiffed up. Amy, you sweep the floors, and John, you go through the rooms after her, and dust everything. I'll wash the windows."

The three of us did a wonderful piece of work. The place looked better than it had for years.

"I am so proud of you. Everything looks perfect, everything in its place. Amy, you changed the sheets on the guest bed, right?"

"Yes I did. You already asked me twice."

"I'm sorry. I'm a little nervous and a little scatterbrained today. "I'm going to have to leave you for a while to meet the lady. Lock the doors and keep them locked until I come back. I'll bring you some candy."

Chapter 53

The Arrival

I sipped a pint at the inn, chewing on jerky and waiting for the coach. It was late, but Arrival time was when the coach actually arrived, not when it was scheduled. I saw Simon at the inn. He always seemed to have time to squander, but he wisely avoided me. I ordered another pint and prepared myself for a long wait.

It must have been my lucky day; she arrived only two and a half hours late. The coach stopped in front of the inn, and four people got out, two men I did not recognize, a boy probably about eight or nine and the most beautiful creature that ever graced the town. I walked toward her while she gathered her bags. She looked around until her eyes stopped on me.

They widened in recognition. "Jacob!"

"Ellie, you are a sight for sore eyes. Welcome home. Let me take your bags to the carriage."

"I didn't expect to see you. Where is George?"

"It was impossible for him to be here."

The boy followed us to the carriage carrying a small bag. She could see I was curious about him.

"This is my son, William Campbell Fitch."

"Pleased to meet you, William. My name is Jacob Morrissey; I'm an old friend of your mother."

"I am pleased to meet you as well, Mr. Morrissey. My mother has told me about you."

"Good things I hope."

"Yes, sir."

"Well, Ellie, he is a handsome young lad."

"Yes, he takes after his father."

"He must be a very handsome man."

"He was. Lieutenant Fitch was killed in the fighting at Fort Schuyler."

"George told me your husband had died. Please accept my condolences."

"Thank you. That's very kind. William never knew him. He was too young. Is this the family carriage?"

"It is. You have a good memory."

"Yes I do. Is Blessed hope in good condition?"

"It is. I believe you will be pleased. How is your mother?"

"She is doing well. She has had a difficult time since my father failed to come back from a mission. She still pines for him, and for Blessed Hope, but I could not persuade her to come with us."

"Oh, excuse me, I almost forgot. I'm supposed to pick up some candy and then we can leave."

She said nothing about our time together before the war until we reached the house. "I remember watching for you to come walking up to the door. You didn't come often enough as far as I was concerned. I also remember the day you walked away and left me forever."

"Those times are gone. Things have changed so much since then. There are so many things to tell you and show you. Come inside. Your room is ready, and the guest room will accommodate William."

We walked to the door, and I knocked. John asked, "Is that you, Uncle?"

"Yes it is. Open the door for us, please."

John's and Amy's attention centered on William. "Who are you?" Amy asked.

"My name is William, but you can call me Will."

"Can you come and play?"

"Just a minute you two. Where are your manners? You haven't even introduced yourselves. And you haven't said hello to William's mother, Ellie"

"I'm John."

"I'm Amy. Now can we go play?"

He looked at his mother. "May I go with them?"

"Yes you may." They were off and out of sight in a flash.

"What beautiful children. Why do they call you Uncle?"

"Because I am their uncle. I am also their Godfather."

"Sit down, Ellie, and I'll fix us some tea. You must be exhausted from your journey."

"I am tired, but I've been sitting so much, I think I would like to stand. Could I just wander around and look at the house while you make the tea?"

"Certainly. Why don't I take your bags upstairs before I start the tea, and you can check your room and William's?"

"That would be just fine."

William will be in George's old room."

"Where does he sleep now? In the master bedroom I suppose?"

I ignored the question. "You check your rooms, and I'll start the tea. Come down when you are ready."

I struggled with how to tell her about her father and brother. I struggled with how much to tell her, but I knew eventually I had to tell her everything. It might destroy her homecoming, and it might destroy any chance that remained for us to put things back together. I needed to do it in the right way; I didn't want it to be any more of a shock to her than it had to be.

The water boiled and I poured it into the pot and let the tea brew. I called up to her. "Ellie, the tea is brewing, are you ready to come downstairs?" Silence.

"Ellie, you can come down now."

I climbed the stairs and walked to her room. The door was open. "Ellie?" I peeked inside. She was on the bed, asleep, and I tip-toed back down.

New Chapter 54

Simon Strikes again

Dinner was ready when the children tore through the house and upstairs, taking a noisy tour.

Ellie came downstairs before the dust settled. "Wow! That was a surprise. I'm not used to three children all at one time. I'm sorry, I must have dozed off."

"It was an hour nap, but you apparently needed it. I didn't have the heart to wake you. I'm reheating the tea. It won't be quite as good as when it was fresh, but it will be hot and refreshing."

She sat at the table, hands folded in front of her. "Jacob, where is George? Why isn't he here?

It had begun. I sucked in a breath and exhaled. "George was killed in the war by the British or Hessians."

"But he promised father he wouldn't join the militia."

"And he kept his promise. He was in Connecticut when the war heated up, and he joined the Connecticut Line. He was a lieutenant in the Continental Army, he was wounded, and he came back to heal and recuperate. He stayed with mother and me, because he didn't want to stay here alone. He was in excellent health when he went back."

"Then what happened?"

"He was promoted to captain and was part of General Washington's staff. He took part in several battles in Pennsylvania and New Jersey, but at Springfield he was severely wounded. He lost an arm and had several other wounds. They brought him back here, and I nursed him. I had the doctor here often, and he was starting to heal, but he didn't want to eat. Then he came down with pneumonia. I did everything the doctor said to do. I had him sitting up, gave him all the fluids he would drink, cooled his head with a towel, but he got worse. I slept by his bed every night, but couldn't save him; he passed away in his sleep."

She sat in quiet reflection, digesting the information. "Where is he buried?"

"His last request was to be buried on the hill under the big oak, and that's what I did."

She was about to ask another question when the door banged several times. I couldn't imagine who it might be. I opened the door, and there stood Simon Tarbell, alcohol breath and all. His bloodshot eyes looked past me at

Ellie. "Did he tell you he killed your father and scalped him?"

My fist came around on its own and smashed into the left side of his ugly face. He stumbled backwards and fell off the steps. I noticed he held up a walking stick in his right hand to ward me off. Its silver handle raised the hackles on my neck. I pounced on him and wrestled the cane away.

"Where did you get this cane, Tarbell?"

His bloody mouth moved, "I bought it."

"Well you better find the person who sold it to you and get your money back. This was stolen from this house. There is a small "WC" right under the lion's head, see? That's William Campbell. I want you off my land, and if I ever see you on it again, I'll carve another notch on my tomahawk."

I watched him get up and walk away before I turned back through the door. As I did, I heard him yell once more. "He let your brother die too."

Ellie stood there with a wild look, the color drained from her face. "Was he telling the truth?"

"Not exactly.

"What does that mean?"

"I believe I shot your father. The militia were in a fight with a raiding party, and I shot at the man who appeared to be their leader. I had no idea it was William. But I did not scalp him. That was a bald faced lie."

"Why did you say, 'get off my property' like you owned it?"

"Because I do. George made me his soul heir when he joined the service. I have a copy of the will, and I have the deed for Blessed Hope."

"How do I know you didn't let him die so you could take over? Simon said you let him die."

"You know I would never have done that. He was my best friend. I did everything possible to save him. It broke my heart when he died."

"If that's all so, why didn't you tell me sooner? I want you to take me and William back to town. I'll find a place for us to stay until I can go back to Canada."

"Stay here. If you still want to leave in the morning, I'll take you to town."

"I'm not going to spend the night in a house with my father's murderer."

"You don't have to. I'll go sleep in the hayloft. The children will be fine. You can lock the doors."

That stopped her for a moment. "Very well. See that you stay there, and don't go thinking I'll change my mind."

****

Sleeping in a hay mow may sound romantic, but your back gets itchy, the dust makes you cough, and it's hard to get comfortable. I slept best the last two hours when exhaustion from tossing, turning, and scratching overtook me.

I woke up to, "Uncle Jacob, Uncle Jacob. Wake up. Will's mother says you need to fix breakfast for us and then you are going to take her and William to town to go back home."

"I'm getting up. Be careful I don't fall on you."

"Why does William have to go? He is so much fun. Is Mrs. Fitch mad at us? We're sorry if we did something she didn't like."

"No, it's not you. It's me. She doesn't like some of the things I did in the war. It's not easy for some people to forgive and forget."

Breakfast was simple, Johnny cake, cold milk and maple syrup. The farm had a wonderful cold spring, the perfect place to keep milk. The only thing colder was Ellie's demeanor; I thought I might get frost bite.

She ate sparingly, and nagged William to eat faster so they could get going. Their bags sat by the door. They had been there when I came in. I wasn't hungry. I hitched up the horse, picked up and loaded their bags, and had them on the road without a word between us. The only conversation was between me and the horse. Her son looked sad, like a whipped puppy.

I pulled up in front of the inn, but no one was around. I got down and checked the coach schedule. "I was afraid of this. You can't leave today; the next coach for Albany is scheduled to arrive at noon tomorrow. We'll go back to Blessed Hope and come back tomorrow."

"We'll stay and get a room at the inn."

"No you won't. It's no place for a lady, and certainly no place for a little boy. Some inns have good accommodations, but this one is sadly lacking, and there is no place else to stay."

"Will you sleep in the hayloft again tonight?"

"If I have to in order to get you to stay, yes I will."

"Why don't you stay with your mother? You would be a lot more comfortable."

"I can't do that."

"You mean, you don't want to do that."

"It doesn't matter. I will be fine in the barn."

New Chapter 55

"I guarantee we won't miss it, but won't you reconsider and stay for a few days. I'll sleep in the haymow. I have so many things I would like to tell you and show you. Please? We can't let everything end this way."

"How can you even think I would stay here with you? You hated my father so much you killed him."

"I didn't know it was your father; his back was to me. If I had recognized him, I would have done my best to spare him. I didn't hate your father, I liked him very much, but I hated the bloody raids that came out of Canada. It was war. Your father warned me that the war would be neighbor against neighbor and friend against friend, and civilians would suffer the most."

"Then they shouldn't have been fighting the King"

"You were safe in Canada; you weren't here to see the real war. It was vicious, ruthless, and terribly destructive. Your father's rangers intended to raid a small community before they withdrew for Canada, but we had information that they were coming, and we were ready for them. We killed three of them and wounded several more before they ran. We caught up with them, and we were in no mood to go easy on them. They put up a good fight, and your father was very brave, but we simply overwhelmed them. Some of the dead Indians had fresh scalps in their pouches. We learned later the group had burned several farms on their way, killing four men, five women and six children. The men we captured said William had tried to stop the warriors from killing the women and children, but failed in his efforts."

I thought that information might mollify her, but instead it only made things worse.

"He was a good man. He didn't deserve to die shot in the back."

"Do you think those five women and six children deserved to die hacked to death and scalped? That wasn't war, it was wholesale murder."

"You shot my father and now you call him a murderer? Have you forgotten how he helped your family when your father died?"

"We could put all the pain behind us and start again."

"No we can't." I want to go home, and I'm going today. Blessed Hope no longer exists for me."

"There's nothing I can say or do to keep you here?"

"Nothing. You are dead to me just like our home. Can't we leave now?"

"In a few minutes. I want to take the children with me. I hate to leave them alone too long."

"Fine, William and I will be in the carriage."

"Would you like to ride into town with us?" I asked them.

"Yes. Can we?"

"I wouldn't have asked if I didn't want you to go."

They ran out and piled into the carriage, and I carried the bags. The children chattered all the way to town, but Ellie answered few questions

"How long will it take you to get home?"

"It depends on when there is a ship going to the Kingston area."

Kingston, I've never heard of it."

"It used to be a little French fort and trading post called Cataraqui."

"Is that where you went when you left?"

"No. We went to Carleton Island first, but after father was killed, we had to move. There wasn't much at Kingston, but some other Loyalist families were already there. When the war ended, Canada began building communities for Loyalists who had lost their homes."

"You and your mother live in Kingston?"

"No."

"Where do you live?"

"In a little village about 12 kilometers west of there."

"Could I come and visit you sometime?"

"No."

"Why not?"

"Because I said no."

"Would you give me your address so I could send you a letter from time to time?"

"No. I don't want you to write. When I saw you waiting for me at the inn, I was ecstatic. I had the foolish notion that we were getting a second chance, but that was romantic nonsense. You were right. Those days are gone. We can't bring them back. Our time has come and gone. Let's just leave it at that."

It was the last word she spoke to me until she said "goodbye" getting into the coach, but she didn't wave.

"Will they come back?" John asked.

"No. I don't think so."

"Why?"

"It's a long story, but basically she doesn't want to."

"That's too bad. We liked William. He was fun to play with."

My stomach felt like I had swallowed a bad mushroom; my head ached like I had been clubbed, and if it hadn't been for Amy and John, I believe I would have gone right then to visit Penelope and Rebecca and join them forever.

New Chapter 56

Where Did I Go Wrong

It's hard to believe, but I had a good night's rest that evening. Maybe because I slept in a bed instead of the haymow. I dreamed of Elizabeth Archer, and the Jecocks' and their farm. Young John fished trout with his grandfather, and Amy made pies in the kitchen with her grandmother, and I saw Elizabeth smiling at them. They disappeared. I viewed Indian bodies and a bloody notched tomahawk, the Canadian Ranger, my first notch, lying on the ground, head split and bloody, my family's graves with flowers, and I was lying across Penelope's grave, my head bloody. I snapped wide awake.

I heard voices. I got dressed, went downstairs and found Amy making oatmeal and John giving culinary advice. The oatmeal was a little thick, and slightly scorched, but once we added milk and spooned maple sugar on it in our bowls, it made a fine breakfast.

"That was very good, Amy. Have you ever thought about making a pie?"

"Grandma Jecocks makes the best pies. She said she would teach me some day."

"Maybe she will, Amy, maybe she will."

I can't explain it, but at that moment nothing made sense anymore. My misery overwhelmed me. I had been depressed before, but now my world was in tatters, and I hated my life. I hated the things I had done and the mistakes I had made. I had thought I could raise the children and I would be fine. I had thought I might even take a wife so they could have a mother, but now I wished I had been killed with Penelope. I wished I could be with her. "You two love your grandmother and grandfather, right?"

"Oh yes." They answered.

"Would you like to spend more time with them?"

"Yes."

The Jecocks' could take care of the children. They would be happy there. If I were gone, they would get over it soon enough. They were young.

"I want you two to pay attention to what I'm telling you. I am going up to my old farm this morning. I want you to stay locked in the house until I get back."

"Can't we go with you?" John asked.

"No. This is something I have to do alone. If I am not back before the sun has gone past its peak, walk to the

Miller home and ask Tom to take you to the doctor's office. Tell him your uncle gave you a note to give to the doctor. If the doctor is not there, wait for him, and give him the note. Do you understand?"

"Yes Uncle Jacob. Are you feeling bad?"

"Don't you worry about me, I'm fine, but don't forget about the doctor. Don't let the sun go down waiting for me, because it's very important you do as I say." As soon as I saddle the horse, I'll come back inside. When I leave, lock the door."

I went to my room and wrote the note for the doctor and sealed it. I returned and handed it to Amy. "Don't open this and don't read it. If you do as I say, you will get to spend some time with grandpa and grandma Jecocks, fishing and baking pies.

I saddled the horse and I told myself I did the right thing. The doctor would see the children got to the Jecocks', and they would be well taken care of there. Amy and John were still in the kitchen when I came back in. "Come here you two, I want to give you a hug."

"Are you crying, Uncle?"

"Maybe a little bit."

"Why?"

"I guess because Ellie is gone and I will never see her again."

I hugged them both, picked up my pistol from the mantle and went out and mounted my horse. They watched me from the porch. I waved, "Don't forget to lock the door, and don't forget the doctor."

I couldn't bear to look back. A slow trot was all that I asked of the horse. We would get there soon enough.

The flowers in Penelope's garden were more gorgeous than I had ever seen them before. The small bench I had made invited me to sit, and I placed my pistol beside me. Thoughts of Mother, Penelope, and Rebecca flooded my mind. We had been so happy. We had so much to live for, and now there was only me.

I should have died several times during the war, but fate decreed that I should survive while all those so close and dear to me did not. Life is sometimes more cruel than death. I became like a ship with no rudder and stripped of sail. I came to discuss my sad state of affairs with my wife.

"Hello Pen. It's been a while, but I didn't forget you. I'll never forget you and Rebecca. The war is over, and I should be happy, but I'm not. I don't feel like farming, I don't feel like anything. Ellie came back a few days ago, and for just a moment, I thought I might be able to build a new life, but it's not to be. She hates me. She has gone back to Canada. She has punished me more than I deserve.

I took in Elizabeth's children. I told you about them the last time I was here, and they gave me some measure of purpose in my life, but they deserve better than me. They will be happier with their grandfather and grandmother. I can see no reason to go on living.

I wrote out a will, leaving Blessed Hope and everything I have to Ellie's son, and she is to be in charge of the estate for him. If she doesn't want to bring her mother back, she can sell it. She said Blessed Hope doesn't exist anymore. I think I understand what she meant.

If no more than Rebecca had been left for me, I could have had hope for the future, but she rests with you, and I shall also ere too long. I shall do what the Redcoats, Royal Yorkers, Canadian Rangers, and Indians were unable to do in eight years of war, and I will find peace."

I picked up my pistol. I had loaded it the evening before, and all I had to do was prime it. I took out my powder and poured some on the pan for ignition, but a thought struck me. What if they take me back and bury me in the church cemetery instead of beside Penelope and Rebecca? That wouldn't do. I should have said in the note.

It was too late to think of that. Too late for everything. I knelt beside the grave, raised the pistol to my head, and pulled the trigger.

Chapter 57

Resurrection

Pain. My head throbbed. Everything was black; I couldn't open my eyes. I tried to figure out where I was and what was wrong with me. My mouth tasted salty. I touched my head where it hurt; it felt sticky. I could tell I was lying on the ground, and I remembered why I was there. It didn't feel like Heaven, and I couldn't be dead; I hurt too much. I heard a voice, "Quit feeling sorry for yourself. Go after her."

It was Pen. I struggled to get up, and wiped my eyes with my sleeve. My eye lashes were sticky and crusty, but I could see. She wasn't there. No one was there. My right sleeve was covered in blood, and I was dizzy. I felt the bench behind my knees and sat down. I was alive.

Something nudged me as I sat. I turned around. My horse nuzzled me again, and I was glad to be alive. Now I feared I would die. I am not sure I could have gotten on the horse without the bench, and once I was in the saddle, I wasn't sure I could stay there, but I had no choice.

What was I thinking? I was so ashamed; I had thought only of myself. I promised Amy and John I wouldn't leave them and then I tried to do it. I hoped I could get back home before they left.

****

Late in the afternoon, I rode into our yard. I knew the children must be in town or on their way. I would have to catch up with them. I had to get the note back, and I turned my mount to head for town and fell off.

Stunned, I heard, "Uncle Jacob. You're hurt. What happened?"

They were still here. Thank God. "I had an accident. Can you help me hitch the horse to the carriage? I need to get to the doctor. You and Amy can come with me."

I felt weaker, and my head tried to explode; I thought I would be sick to my stomach. The ride to the doctor was anything but pleasant. The only good thing was we found the doctor at home.

"Good Lord, Jacob, let me help you." He said as he pulled my arm over his shoulder and put his arm around my back. I wobbled all the way into his office, and he helped me up onto his table.

"You children need to go out into my waiting room until I am done with your Uncle."

"Is he going to die?" Asked John.

"No, I don't think so. I'll call you in when we are finished." He closed the door behind them.

"What in heaven's name happened to you?"

"I had an accident."

"What sort of accident?"

"I dropped my pistol and it went off somehow."

"Hmm. Well, let me check the wound, clean it and wrap it up."

When he finished, he asked me, "How did you say this happened?"

"I dropped my pistol and it went off."

"That's strange. It's almost impossible for that to happen, and I see powder burns in your hair. Want to tell me what's going on? Did someone try to kill you?"

It took me some time to tell him what happened and why. He thought about it, "Do you still want to kill yourself?"

"No."

"Good. You are fortunate; you have a second chance at life in more ways than one, and I wish you luck on your quest. But if you do decide to shoot yourself again, make sure you have a ball in the barrel."

"What do you mean?"

"Well, there couldn't have been a ball in your gun or you'd be dead. You shot yourself with wadding. It was enough to be painful and rip up your scalp, and make a mess, but you've got a thick skull, and it didn't penetrate enough to be mortal. Keep it clean and you will heal up completely in two to three weeks."

"Am I well enough to travel?"

"I suggest you wait two days before you go anywhere. After that, if you feel well enough go ahead, but don't overdo, and keep the wound clean."

I used the two days wisely. I hugged the children and swore I would never leave them alone again. We talked about their grandparents, and I asked them if they would like to spend some time with them, like we had talked about earlier. "Yes we would love to go." They assured me.

"I am going to take you to see them, but there is something I have to do if you agree. I need to find Ellie and see if I can talk her into coming back. No matter what, I will come back for you after I've seen her. Will you be good and wait for me to get back? It may take me quite a while to find her."

"If you find her, will she come back and be our mother?"

"I hope so. I'll do my best, but she may not come with me."

"How long will you be gone?"

"I'm not sure. Probably about five to seven weeks, but possibly a little longer. I have to get passage to Kingston, and then I have to find her, before I can start back. What do you think? How do you feel about it? I won't go if you are afraid."

I was proud of them. They discussed it like adults before they answered. "We don't want you to go, but we want you to be happy. We liked William and Mrs. Fitch. We hope they will come back. Please come back as quickly as you can."

"I won't leave you any longer than is absolutely necessary, and you won't be alone you will be with family. That's very important."

Chapter 58

Destination Canada

We arrived at the Jecocks home without incident. Harold could hardly believe his eyes when he opened his door. He recovered quickly. "Amelia, we have company, come and see."

"Oh my goodness. Come over here and give grandma a big hug."

Amy and John rushed over to her and she smothered them in her arms. "What a surprise. Grandpa and I were talking about you this morning and here you are."

"Harold asked, "How long are you here for?"

"I'm not going to be here long, but I'm hoping you will be willing to watch these little whirlwinds for a couple months."

"What do you think, Amelia, can we handle these two while Jacob is gone?"

"It will be wonderful. I'd love to spoil them for you. Where are you going anyway?"

"I'm going to Canada, but first I'm going to Albany to take care of some business. I'll stop back here when I'm finished there, and then I'm going on to Oswego."

"Have the British turned it over to us? I understood they were refusing to leave."

"It's still under their control, and there is a good reason. Thousands of Loyalists are going to Canada from the port in Oswego. I'm planning to go as one myself. It's a lot easier and less costly than to go to New York and take a ship from there. They will never know I was in the Militia."

"Will you come back the by the same route?"

"If I can. If not, I'll go the long way. I hope the children will not be a burden for you."

"Don't you trouble yourself about that; there are chores that John can help me with, and I'm pretty sure Amelia can't wait to get Amy into the kitchen."

"They will love it. Amy makes great oatmeal. She scorched some for us just before we left."

****

My journey to Albany was successful. I had accomplished the second part of my plan and returned to the Jecocks. Amy and John cornered me first thing and told me about the things they had been doing while I was away. Amy said, "I'll cook for you when you come home. Grandma is going to teach me. She showed me how to make pie crust, and how to put flour and sugar in with the berries. I made two berry pies yesterday. John ate half of one, but there is a whole one left for today."

It was excellent. I took a piece of it with me when I left the next day. I took the carriage back to Blessed Hope, and put it in the barn. I took some of the money from the library hide away, and I rode the horse to Oswego. I planned to sell the horse and tackle when I got there.

I met a Loyalist from Virginia who was headed to Canada with his horse. "Why are you taking your horse with you?"

He looked at me like I was daft. "He's my horse. Why wouldn't I take him with me?"

"I thought I would sell mine."

"If you aren't fond of your horse, sell him once you get to Canada, but not here. You will get at least five pounds more. But I am keeping mine. He served me faithfully during the war."

I almost said, "Are you a Loyalist?" But I stopped myself, and asked, "Who did you serve with?"

"I was in the Militia. Some of the time we were with Lord Cornwallis, but weren't with him at Yorktown. Who were you with?"

"Johnson's Royal Yorker's."

"Are you planning to settle near Kingston?"

"I have friends there. Mrs. Ruth Campbell and her daughter, Ellie. Their father was Captain William Campbell of the Royal Yorkers. He died during the war, and I wanted to talk with them about him."

"I wish you success with your visit."

I learned several men planned to take their mounts with them, so I decided to take mine, and it was not difficult to find a ship that could accommodate us and take us to Kingston. I had never sailed before, and I got miserably ill, seasick I was told. My fellow passengers thought it was amusing, but I thought I would die before we reached land. My horse seemed unaffected by the motion of the ship, but I think he was as relieved as I was when we got off the ship.

I found a place where I could get out of the sun and sit down. I had a headache, but my nausea seemed to dissipate once I was on solid ground. I was convinced I could never sail all the way from Kingston to New York City; they would have to bury me at sea. I located a livery stable and made arrangements for the care and feeding of my horse, and found a room in a nearby inn.

I struck up a conversation with the innkeeper. "I understand there is land for loyalists west of here. Is that true?"

"Yes, quite a few of you fellows are coming through here. Some stay, others go west, and the rest spread out to join friends."

"Would you happen to know Mrs. Ruth Campbell and her daughter, Ellie, by any chance?"

"No. I've never met them."

"Did you ever hear of Captain William Campbell?"

"Not that I can remember."

It would have been too much to expect that the first person I asked would know them, but I was determined to start heading west and ask anyone I met. Sooner or later I would find someone who knew her. It would have been so much easier if she had given me the settlement name.

Chapter 59

Searching for Ellie

I encountered scattered homes soon after leaving Kingston, and each one tempted me to stop, but Ellie had said they were about twelve kilometers west of the small city. I rode on until I figured I had gone at least eight kilometers and stopped at the next home I saw. I tethered my horse and walked to the door.

The owner came to the door. The first thing he said was, "We don't have any extra food."

"I'm not looking for food; I'm looking for a family. Do you know Ruth Campbell?"

"Sorry young man. Never heard of her."

Each time I stopped, the answers I received disappointed me, but I continued on. It seemed like I must have traveled at least sixteen kilometers or more by midday. I wondered if I might have passed the area where their home was located.

I expected another failure when I stopped at the next house and knocked at the door. "Hello, sir, I am wondering if you could help me. I am trying to find Ruth Campbell. Do you know of her?"

"Does she have a daughter named Ellie?"

Ellie's name gave my heart a lift and my voice rose in pitch and speed. "Yes she does. Do you know where I can find them?"

"Why are you looking for them?"

"I am a friend of the family. I knew Captain Campbell quite well."

"He was a good loyalist. He's dead, you know."

"Yes I do know that. It saddened me greatly."

"They live not far from here. Continue down the road about a kilometer and you will see the path to their section. There is a clump of three white birches standing right where the path leaves the road."

"Thank you so much, sir. They will be surprised to see me."

The directions led me right to their home. It wasn't much compared to their home in Tryon County. Times must have been hard for them after William was gone. I took a deep breath, walked up to the door and knocked. There was no answer. I knocked again, louder. The door opened and Ruth stood before me.

She looked at me for a few moments and said, "Jacob?"

"Yes, it's me."

"Is Ellie here?"

"No. She took William to the doctor."

"May I come in?"

"Yes. It may surprise you, but I expected you would come."

"I am surprised."

"Sit down and I will get us a spot of tea."

I looked around as I waited. The house was sparsely furnished, giving the impression of frugality or simply impoverishment. I found it depressing to see them in such circumstances.

"Here's your tea. I have no sugar for it, I'm afraid."

"That's fine. I don't use anything in my tea."

"Elspeth told me about her visit. Would you mind if I ask you a few questions?"

"Not at all. I came to talk."

"She said you killed my husband. Is that true?

"I believe that to be true."

"Would you tell me how it happened?"

I described the battle and told her I did not know who I was shooting at.

"Mrs. Campbell, do you remember Simon Tarbell? He told Ellie that I had killed William and scalped him, and

I guess she believes him instead of me. I told her I didn't scalp him."

"I never learned what happened to his body. Do you know?"

"Yes. I brought him home. He is buried on the rise overlooking Blessed Hope. Please don't tell Ellie. I have my reasons"

"Elspeth said Simon had accused you of letting George die when he was wounded and under your care. She said you claimed that he left our home to you in his will. Is that true?"

"I took care of him, and the doctor checked on him almost every day. I didn't let him die; he got pneumonia and the doctor and I couldn't save him.

George gave me a copy of his will naming me the executor of his estate, and his beneficiary. I tried to change his mind, but he was adamant. The only thing he wanted was that I would invite you and Ellie to return and live there. I had no idea how to find you until Ellie came to visit him and found me instead."

"She said you practically begged her to stay. Is that true?"

"Again, yes, that is true, but she refused to listen and left."

"Why have you come?"

"Because I love her. I want to persuade her to come back and bring you with her. I would like to marry her, but I can live with the disappointment if she wants nothing to do with me. Before I came, I signed the deed to Blessed hope over to Master William Campbell, and Ellie is to be in charge of the estate and his affairs until he is eighteen. I never had a desire to own it, but George wouldn't listen to me."

"It may surprise you again, Jacob, but I believe everything you have told me. I could not accept the thought that you had killed my husband because you hated him, and I was convinced you would never have scalped him.

Certainly if you had schemed to get Blessed Hope, you would not have gone to the trouble to give it away to William and my daughter. I am on your side in this, and I believe my husband would be as well if he could tell us. It grieved him for taking Elspeth away from you, and I don't think she ever completely forgave him for it."

"Thank you for that. I am relieved that you understand and believe me. I would like to stay and talk with Ellie and try to persuade her to come back."

"As much as you would like to do that, I urge you to leave without seeing her. Give me the opportunity to reason with her. I think that would be more successful.

Send us a message as soon as you can with the information about the disposition of Blessed Hope. That might be the key to changing her mind.”

“If she still refuses, may I come and visit you again and speak with her?”

“I would be pleased to see you again in any case.”

Chapter 60

Will she come?

I made one stop on my way back to pick up the children. I knew they all would be surprised and excited to have me back, but I wanted to write a letter to Ruth and Ellie and get it on its way as quickly as possible. After that, I could spend a few days with family and rest from my journey.

The children were in the yard and saw me before I got to the house. They ran down the road, "Uncle Jacob, you're back, you're back. Uncle Jacob, Uncle Jacob."

I stopped the horse. "Hop in you two."

I got hugs and kisses and all sorts of questions. John asked, "Are Ellie and William going to come back?"

Amy said, "Can we stay a little longer?"

"Wait a minute. One question at a time. I don't know if Ellie and William are coming back. I hope so, but I don't know yet. Yes we can stay a little longer if your Grandmother and grandfather don't mind."

"Was it fun to sail across the lake?"

"I'll never forget it."

"Did you bring us anything?"

"No, I'm sorry, but I didn't find anything for children."

I pulled into the yard and Harold came outside. "Welcome home. You are back a lot sooner than you expected to be. How did you do?"

"I had an interesting trip. I found the family and had a good conversation with Ruth. Ellie was at the doctor's with William. I left without talking to her."

"I thought that was why you went. Did her mother discourage you?"

"No. Just the opposite, she said she was on my side, and that it would be best to let her reason with Ellie. I know where they live now, so I can go back and see Ellie if Ruth fails. I'll have to wait and see."

"Are you leaving right away?"

"I thought I would stay for 3 or 4 days if you don't mind."

"Heaven's no. I don't mind and the Mrs. Will be overjoyed. Come on in."

****

We had a great time together and I wanted to stay almost as much as the children, but I needed to be home when the message came from Canada. I thought about leaving Amy and John there, so I asked them if they would like that.

"No we want to go home. We had a good time, but we miss our home."

"I didn't have the heart to tell them that the place they called home might not be our home any longer. It would be tough enough when the day came; there was nothing to be gained by upsetting them with it at that time.

"I miss it too, but you know what? I'm going to rebuild my cabin where your mother is buried. You can help me build it. What do you think?"

Amy's response was less than enthusiastic, but John was ready to start the next day. "Can I work on the roof?"

"We'll see. Now let's get started, the sooner we get home, the sooner we can get to building."

The die was cast, and I was sure we were living at Blessed Hope on borrowed time. I assembled the items I needed to start work on the cabin, but somehow I couldn't get myself going. I began to think that Ellie had not been swayed by her mother. About the time that I considered another trip to Canada, seasickness or no, her letter arrived.

"Jacob, Mother has made it clear to me that she intends to go back to Blessed Hope, with or without me. I am forced to go with her, but I don't like it at all. She told me you have signed Blessed Hope over to us. If that is really true, I will accept it, but do not expect that you will live there, even in the barn. My mother is willing to forgive you, but I have not.

You may expect us on the 24th. Mother told me how you had come across from Oswego, and that is a less arduous journey and much less expensive than sailing to New York. Oswego is held by the British, so we should have no problems there.

When we arrive, or before if possible, please move your possessions from our property. I am sure your mother will welcome you back. The carriage belongs to Blessed Hope, so I expect you will leave it there. All other matters we can discuss and settle when we arrive.

Please be at our home when we arrive. Respectfully yours,

Elspeth

Campbell

Fitch

It was hardly the warmest letter I had ever received, but she was coming. I might not win her over, but at least she would be back where she belonged. It was time for me to explain to the children what was going to happen.

"Come into the kitchen, there is something I need to tell you."

"What is it?"

"When Ellie gets here, we have to move out."

"Why?"

"Because I have given the farm back to her family."

"Why?"

"Because I don't feel right about keeping it. It belonged to their family before the war."

"Where will we go?"

"For the time being I will take you back to your grandparents until I have the cabin built, and then I will come and get you."

"Why is she making us go?"

"I told you before, it's not you, it's me, but she can't send me packing without my taking you with me."

"William is going to be sad. He won't have anyone to play with."

"Maybe when the cabin is done, he can come and visit us once in a while."

"She's not going to be our mother?"

"Doesn't look like it. I'm sorry. I did the best I could."

"Now you two go outside and play and I'll fix something for dinner."

****

341

Ruth, Ellie, and William arrived at eleven in the morning on the 24th. Ellie was aloof, but Ruth gave me a hug, and her grandson took off with Amy and John. "It looks as beautiful as the day we left it. You kept it up well, Jacob."

"Thank you Mrs. Campbell. Just so you know, the winter's firewood is all split and stacked, and the winter wheat is in the ground so you will have a harvest in the spring. There are about fourteen laying hens, and three hens are sitting somewhere. There are basic items in the pantry, and there is a ham in the smokehouse."

I took the papers out of the library hiding place, and handed them to Ellie. Here is the deed to the property all signed and witnessed. Put it somewhere safe. I have a favor to ask of you. I would like your permission to put my belongings in your barn for a short time, and I would like you to allow the children to stay here for about two weeks. Then we will get out of your way.

"I have a gentleman friend coming in about three weeks. I would like to have everything cleaned up and in good order by then. Why don't you take your belongings and the children to your mother's cabin? There should be room enough."

Chapter 61

It stung worse than a white-faced hornet. Ruth hadn't said anything about another man, and Ellie didn't seem very appreciative of the deed. She had no sympathy with my request.

"Ellie, there is something you need to see, and if you want me and the children out of here today, you had better come with me to see my mother. Let me harness the horse and hook up the carriage."

Ruth had been listening, and before Ellie could answer, she said, "Elspeth, you need to go with him, or I am going to live with his family instead of here with you."

She was taciturn, looking away from me as we rode to see mother. When I stopped on the cabin side of the rise, she looked around. "What happened to your cabin?"

"The Indians and British burned it to the ground."

I gave the horse a slight slap of the reins and he moved down the hill. I pulled him up at the flowers. "Get down." I didn't help her.

"I brought you to see mother, and the cabin you want me to move into. See the markers? The first one is Elizabeth Archer. The Indians killed her and burnt her home in 1782. The war was basically over, but the British were still paying the Indians for scalps. Next to her is my mother, next is my wife Penelope and our beautiful baby daughter. The three of them were killed by Indians and British in 1778. Our daughter, Rebecca, was less than two years old. She had beautiful curly hair. The Indians tomahawked her and scalped her. I went crazy for a while.

"That's what the loyalists and Indians were doing on their glorious raids. Killing their old friends and neighbors and their infant children."

She was silent.

"Get in the carriage, we are going back to Blessed Hope. There is something else I need to show you."

She remained quiet riding back, but she looked down, not off to the side. I pulled into the wagon path beside Blessed Hope. "Get down." Her mother watched from the doorway.

Ellie looked at me, "What happened to my father's body after he was killed. Did someone else scalp him?"

"No, I wouldn't allow it. There is something more you need to see. Let's walk up the hill to where George is buried."

As we neared the top and the big oak tree, we could see two wooden markers. "Who else is buried here?"

"When I shot your father, I brought him all the way back here, washed him and his uniform, put it back on him and buried him. He died first. When your brother died, I washed him, put his new uniform on, and buried him under the oak, because he requested I do that. I buried them next to each other because I cared about them. Can't you understand I loved them both? The Patriot and the Loyalist. I laid them to rest on this hill, your father's favorite spot, where they could always look on Blessed Hope together. I talked with your mother, and she asked me to promise I would bury her next to her husband. I promised. I never hated your father, none of you."

She read the markers, "Captain William Campbell, His Majesty's Royal Yorkers" and "Captain George Campbell, Connecticut Line, Continental Army"

"Why didn't you tell me all of this when I was here before?"

"You wouldn't let me. You were too upset by what Tarbell said. Come, I will take you back down to the house."

"Not yet. I see father's bench is still here. Would you sit with me while I look at our home with my family?"

"Of course, for as long as you like."

I jumped when she took my hand. Tears slid down her cheeks. I felt bad for her, and I knew, no matter what, I could not live without this woman by my side.

"Ellie, will you marry me, and be the mistress of Blessed hope?"

"Oh, Jacob, I can't. I'm already engaged to a man in Canada."

"I'm here, he is there, and all is fair in love and war. Can't you just tell him you have changed your mind?"

"I'm not sure that would be fair to him."

"Then be fair to yourself. Consider this, it comes from Shakespeare. 'To thine own self be true.' I have always lived by it. If you truly love him, run to him, but if you truly love me, marry me, or for the rest of your life you will be living a lie."

"Jacob, I have thought about you every day of my life since the hay mow, even while I was married. I was ashamed of myself, but I couldn't help it. I didn't want to let myself think about you after I found out about father. It seemed unfair to him to love you. There is something else I haven't told you. William is named after his grandfather."

"That sounds like a reasonable choice to me. So what is his full name?"

"William Tiberius."

"Tiberius?"

"Yes, he's your son. He's a Morrissey."

"Are you sure?"

"Positive. You gave me a precious going away present. I was carrying William before I married Lieutenant Fitch. Father insisted I marry him for the family's honor, but there is no question, he is yours."

"Then we have to get married, we already have a family. Do you think your mother will stay here and live with us?"

"Why not? She loves you too."

"Are you saying you will marry me?"

"Yes. When I was thirteen, I told my mother I was going to marry you, and I will. I'll be Mrs. Elspeth Morrissey, the mistress of Blessed Hope."

Leon Archer is a retired high school library media specialist and is the longtime author of The Sportsman's World column in the Valley News. He has been a lifelong student of history, and weaves a tapestry of romance and days long past.

You can find more of Leon Archer's work at www.jacolpublishing.com

9 781946 675361